THE
CASTLE
KEY

Karen Krossing

Napoleon Publishing

Text © 2000 by Karen Krossing

Cover art: Chrissie Wysotski

Le Conseil des Arts du Canada depuis 1957 | The Canada Council for the Arts since 1957

We gratefully acknowledge the support of the Canada Council for the Arts for our publishing program.

Napoleon Publishing
Toronto, Ontario, Canada

Printed in Canada

05 04 03 02 01 00   5 4 3 2 1

Canadian Cataloguing in Publication Data

Krossing, Karen, date
  The castle key

ISBN 0-929141-76-8

I. Title

PS8571.R776C37 2000   jC813'.6   C00-931951-4
PZ7.K935Ca   2000

To Kevin, who always believed
even when I forgot how.

To Paige, Tess, Katherine and Megan.
May you find your magic.

AUTUMN IN THE YEAR 1250

Nora lifted her gown slightly as she raced down the curved stone stairway. Noises from outside in the courtyard urged her on—hooves of war horses pounding the earth, swords clashing and the screams of dying men.

The slam of a thick wooden door echoed through the stairwell. Moments later, Nora reached for its smooth metal handle.

"Open the door," she called, tugging desperately.

But she heard no reply.

"Please, let me through!" Nora banged on the rough wooden planks until her fists were raw with slivers.

When the knight first found her, he did not realize who his prize was. He was breathless and blinded by the rage of battle. But once he had wiped the sweat and blood from his face, he laughed hoarsely through his cracked and broken teeth.

"You have lived to see twelve winters, Eleanora of Stedmere," he growled. "But you will live to see no more."

A shiver passed through Nora as she pressed herself against the door. Fear left her then, as she faced her death.

The knight's sword found its mark, piercing her chest with a quick thrust. He shouted with the fever of revenge. Nora gasped then slumped to the ground. The intruder pulled his sword free and wiped it on her cloak.

Soon, a ghostly glow rose from Nora's body, although the knight did not see it. The ghost of Nora peeled away from the broken form and hovered confused before the knight as he slipped on his helmet.

"Am I alive or dead?" she wondered.

Her murderer was deaf to her ghostly whispers, but, as if in answer to her question, he gloated as he stepped over Nora's body and turned back to the stairs: "A bitter death for your father's sins."

Nora glided after him as he stomped back up the stairs into the fighting that still raged throughout the inner courtyard. The glow that was Nora moved up the spiral stairs to the top of the tower.

At the tower window, Nora watched with dull eyes as the attackers destroyed most of the castle and burned all the wooden buildings within the castle walls.

"Cursed be the enemies of my father." She screamed the words, but no one could hear her.

A gust of autumn wind breezed through the narrow window, although it could not touch her. Nor could she feel the press of the cool stone wall against her cheek. She drew her cloak tightly around her and pulled her hood over her head. Yet this too offered no comfort.

Hours passed, but Nora hovered still on the tower above the battlefield that had been her home, staring as if in a trance at the scene below her. Then, slowly, a power swelled in her until she surged with light, enough to be seen by the eyes of the living, if any were there who looked on high toward the tower. The sky darkened over the castle as angry clouds gathered. The wind whipped with such force that rocks in the castle wall were shaken loose. Then lightning flashed, and the rain began to pour down in thick sheets.

Shaking with her sudden strength, Nora turned her face toward the sky and spoke with the fury of one who had been wronged. She spoke with such passion, such faith, that her words were like daggers hurled from her lips.

"Cursed be those who abandoned me."

Her light dimmed as the curse emptied from her. But her sorrowful shade remained to haunt the castle ruins through the ages.

1

MOON MAGIC

Have you ever wondered what colours would sound like, if they had a sound? I first heard the colour blue on a rainy Saturday afternoon when my friend Duncan and I were messing around with magic. It was a soft tinkle like a tiny bell that brought to mind the cornflower blue of a summer sky, and I thought of the sapphire ring that my mother had given me on the day she left.

Duncan and I were hiding from the rain in the shabby apartment I shared with my Dad. It was quieter than Duncan's house— a better place to try magic. But I hated the drab beige and brown of this apartment we moved into after my mother left. I wanted to paint it bright colours, but my father wanted the colours in his life to be dull.

Dad was at work, as usual. And we were

hanging out in my room, since it was less depressing than the rest of the place. I had plastered the beige walls with photos of me with my smiling Mom and Dad.

"Let's use magic to find my mother," I said hopefully. I believed in magic, and Duncan wanted to believe in magic. But we hadn't made it work for us yet.

"We could try," Duncan agreed. He pushed his straight dark hair out of his face. His matching dark brown eyes were like deep mud puddles.

Even though Duncan and I go to the same school, we never really became friends until the night of the magic show at our school the year before. It wasn't real magic—just stage magic to amuse kids. Tricks of the eye performed badly by a deadbeat old guy who sucked his teeth. After each trick, I whispered to Duncan how he had done it. Duncan told me that he was fascinated by magic too. From that moment, we were magic partners.

"We'll use wishing magic." I held up a tall, narrow candle I had taken from the living room. "I'll write my wish on a piece of paper and put it under this candle. Then we'll burn the candle completely, thinking about the wish the whole time."

"That candle will take hours to burn," said Duncan. "We should use the kind of candle you put on a birthday cake. Do you have any of those, Moon?"

Moon—that's my name. My Mom chose it because I was born at midnight on the night of a full moon. She said the moon was the first thing she saw after she looked at her new baby girl. Then she noticed that on my cheek was a crescent-shaped birthmark, just like a quarter moon. So she called me Moon.

"I'll check the kitchen." Then I ran to get the leftover candles from my twelfth birthday eight months ago.

"Got some," I said as I hurried back into my room. Duncan was wandering around staring at the photos on the wall.

I grabbed a couple of pens and some paper off my desk. "Here, you can make a wish too." I shoved a pen and paper at Duncan. He took them from me, but a slight frown passed across his face.

We wedged ourselves on the floor between my dresser, bed and desk. I wrote "I want to find my mother" on a piece of paper and showed it to Duncan. But he hadn't written anything yet.

"I don't know what to wish for," he said, when he caught me looking at him.

I thought about it. Maybe Duncan didn't have that much to wish for. He had an almost perfect life in an almost perfect family.

"You could wish for a new computer," I suggested.

Duncan was a computer nut. He practically lived on the Internet some days, only coming out for food. Last year he had wanted a cell phone so he could check his e-mail messages hourly, but his Mom had vetoed that. Of course, he already had his own computer in his room. But considering that his Mom was a computer programmer, maybe he could get a better one.

"Maybe I'll just watch," he said.

I let out a big sigh then leaned back against the colourful Mexican blanket that covered my bed. It was a special treasure— my Mom had bought it for me.

"Why won't you try?" I asked.

"I don't know," he said simply.

"Are you afraid that the magic might work?"

"No." He pressed his lips together tightly.

I gave him a hard up-and-down look.

Duncan hung his head to avoid my eyes,

but I knew he could still feel me glaring at him. "Okay, Moon. I guess I'll wish for a new computer."

"Great." I watched him write out his wish.

Then I melted some wax on the bottom of a white candle and stood it up in a small dish I'd brought from the kitchen. I folded the two papers under the dish on the floor between us.

"Think of it as a birthday wish," I suggested. "Before you blow out the candles on your cake, you make a wish, right? And if you can think of it clearly and hold the wish in your mind, it will happen. Maybe not quite how you imagined it would, but it will happen."

Duncan nodded at me, but he didn't look too sure.

I lit the candle and said:

"Candle burn and magic grow
I write this wish to make it so.
Candle burn so clear and white,
Guide our magic toward the light."

"Where did you get that?" Duncan asked.

"Shh. I made it up." Then Duncan knew to be quiet.

The rain pounded at my bedroom window. A heavy silence lay between us. I tried to focus on our wishes, and I hoped Duncan was trying too. Then I heard the bell.

The tinkle of the bell was so soft at first that my ears barely caught it. Then it grew louder, although it was still a thin wisp of noise. As if tiny elves were ringing delicate glass bells that faintly sounded the colour blue.

I looked at Duncan to see if he could hear it too, but he was staring intently at the candle. I guess he was trying to make the magic work. But I knew he hadn't heard the bell.

My stomach twirled in delighted somersaults, and my heart beat doubletime. Was it true? I'd been waiting for years to work magic. Ever since my mother first wove me tales of magic each night before bed, I'd been hoping. For proof. For real magic. And now, had I found it?

I gasped with pleasure. Duncan knew something had happened. He stared nervously at me with wide, surprised eyes.

"What is it, Moon?" he whispered.

"I heard a bell. It sounded blue," I whispered back. I was afraid to shatter the magic.

"Oh, Moon. This is too weird for me."

Duncan's pale face grew even paler. He looked over his shoulder as if he thought someone or something was standing behind him.

"Did you ever wonder what blue sounds like?" I asked.

"Never," he answered.

Then I caught a flash of blue reflected in the mirror above my dresser.

I jumped up to peer into the glass. "Did you see that?"

"What?"

The blue was gone. I stared at my reflection. Short dark hair like a boy's brush cut. Blue eyes the colour of sapphires. Chipped front tooth and a crooked smile.

Then Duncan was beside me, leaning on the dresser and squinting into the mirror. His straight hair fell into his eyes as if he was trying to hide from something.

"What are you looking at?" he asked into the mirror.

"I heard a bell that sounded like blue then I saw a flash of blue, like the sapphire ring I lost the day my Mom left."

"Oh." He nodded slowly. "I didn't see anything." He peeked out from beneath his hair. I think he hadn't decided yet if it was safe to come out.

But I was barely listening to him. The bell tinkled softly again. And I was swept back into my painful memories of the day my mother left. It was the day of my twelfth birthday—September 21. The first day of autumn. A day of balance, when the night and day are equal. After that, the nights get longer and longer until, finally, the darkness rules over the light of day—just as my life had become darker and darker since that fateful day.

2

THE RING

I remembered waking on the day of my twelfth birthday with a glorious feeling of warmth. The sun shone through the window in the house we used to rent, rousing me with tender fingers of light. My mother stood tall and thin at the end of my bed, her piercing blue eyes just like mine and her dark auburn hair like a burned-out sun.

"Get up, birthday girl. I have a surprise for you." Her face shone as she spoke.

I didn't need to be asked twice. I scrambled out of bed and bounced over to my Mom for a birthday hug. I squeezed her tightly, but she pushed my arms away. "Enough, Moon."

My mother didn't like to be hugged, although she did show her love by pulling Dad and me into her adventures. Life was always fireworks when she was around.

"Shut your eyes, hold out your hands, and don't peek," she ordered. "Remember what'll happen if you peek? Your birthday present will mysteriously vanish in a puff of smoke." My mother gave the same warning every year.

I giggled, but I kept my eyes squeezed shut. There was no use in taking any chances. I felt my Mom place a small box in my hands. "Can I look now?" I begged.

"Okay. You can look." My mother let out a short laugh.

I opened my eyes to a small green gift box. "Can I open it?" But I didn't wait for her answer. Inside was nestled a silver ring with a large blue sapphire that sparkled in the morning light.

"Oh, Mom. It's so beautiful," I whispered.

My mother quickly squeezed my hand. "I'm glad you like it, Moon." Then her voice grew strangely quiet. "It isn't just a ring, you know. It's a talisman. It has special powers."

I looked curiously at my Mom. I had never seen her so still and serious.

"The sapphire is your birthstone—your lucky stone. Wear it every day for protection. It will ward off evil and bring you good fortune. Here, read the words on the inside."

I held the ring up to the sunlight to read the tiny letters. "'Choose belief over doubt.' What does that mean?"

But she didn't give me any real answer. "This ring is my special gift to you. Keep it with you always." She slid the ring onto my finger.

"I will," I replied with the same serious tone as my mother. "I promise." And I meant it.

Then my Dad appeared at Mom's shoulder. "Happy birthday, Moon." He leaned around Mom and brushed a kiss on my cheek. I saw Mom stiffen at his touch. Then Dad noticed the ring. "Wow. Isn't that a little fancy for a young girl to wear, Jane? Maybe she should save it for special occasions."

"But I'm twelve," I objected.

"No way, David," my mother said at the same time. "I didn't give it to her so it could sit in a box. This ring is for everyday and everywhere. You'll be careful with it, won't you, Moon?"

"Of course, Mom. I'll be very careful. Really, Dad. Can I wear it, please?"

My father was not about to start an argument with my mother. He sensed that the ring was special. "Sure, Moon. Just don't lose it." His words rang out like a warning.

Twelve was really too old for a party, but we did invite Duncan to a special birthday lunch at my favourite Chinese restaurant. On the way back to the car, it was raining hard. He lent me his jacket so my grown-up silk blouse wouldn't get soaked. My mother smiled at this gesture.

"Quite the gentleman," she commented. I rolled my eyes at her, and Duncan ducked his head.

At home we finished off the celebration with chocolate cake and pecan ice cream. Only after Duncan had left for home did I notice that my ring was missing.

I cried until I had no more tears. We looked in every nook and cranny—all through the house and in the car. We phoned every place we'd stopped by that day. But it was nowhere to be found. My mother was as upset as I was.

That night, I woke to the muffled voices of my parents arguing. The voices stilled; a door clicked closed. Sleep pulled me back, and I didn't wake until late the next morning. By then, my mother was gone.

Dad held me tight and said, "I don't think

she's coming back. But she did leave you a note."

I opened the envelope and quickly read her scratchy, hurried handwriting. "I have given you all I can. Love, Mom." That was all.

I cried. I didn't think I could live without her. And I felt her leaving was my fault for losing the ring. I had brought the bad luck.

Dad tried to comfort me. "We'll manage, Moon. We'll make a new family, just the two of us."

But I could tell that he didn't really think we could. He looked really worn out and hopeless. His clothes were wrinkled and his head looked too heavy for him to lift. How were we going to manage on our own?

Ever since that day I'd felt as if a piece of myself were missing. As if I had a huge, gaping hole inside me that ached to be filled.

"Moon?" Duncan was calling me.

"Huh?" I answered. "What did you say?"

He was staring at our faces in the mirror, his forehead wrinkled with worry.

"You just spaced out there. What's going on?"

"I don't know." I shook my head slowly. I was still confused by my memories but excited about the magic of the bell.

Another bell chimed. Another flash of blue across the surface of the mirror. And my head was spinning with the glorious sound of magic.

I saw Ms. Tanglemoth, the librarian at our school. Her cotton dress hung loosely on her thin frame. Her grey hair was pulled into a tight bun on her head, and a pencil poked out from behind her ear. She held something in her hands—something very precious. But I couldn't make out what it was. Then I was back in my room again with Duncan.

I turned to look at the candle. It had burned all the way down. Only a faint trail of smoke hovered above a puddle of wax.

Duncan seemed agitated. "I don't know what's going on. But I don't see your mother or a new computer anywhere." He tried to laugh as if it were a joke.

I ignored his words. "I've got to see Ms. Tanglemoth," I said to him with amazement.

"What?" Duncan seemed more bewildered than ever. "Why her? And it's Saturday."

"Monday is so far away." I groaned. Then

I sat up straighter. "Well, not today then. But right after school on Monday, we're going to see Ms. Tanglemoth."

Duncan shuddered. "But Ms. Tanglemoth is a witch! She answers my questions before I even ask them!"

"We have to go see her," I insisted. "I'm not sure why, but I know that we have to go see her."

3

MS. TANGLEMOTH

On Monday after school, Duncan and I met outside the double doors to the library. I was there first, pacing restlessly in circles on the square floor tiles. Of course, I could have gone in without him, but I wanted him with me for moral support.

I didn't have to wait long. "You ready?" I asked him as soon as he appeared.

He walked toward me with slow steps. "I guess so."

But neither one of us moved to go in.

We were both more than a little bit nervous. Like Duncan, I suspected Ms. Tanglemoth was a witch. And not only because she could be mean and crafty, but because she seemed to know things about people without having been told. Secret things that she shouldn't know.

"What are we looking for, anyway?" Duncan asked.

"I don't know. I just know we have to go in there."

Duncan didn't say anything.

"Let's go," I said, trying to be brave. We swung open the orange metal doors and marched in together.

Ms. Tanglemoth was guarding one side of the entrance from behind her large wooden desk. On the other side, tall and skinny Marta and another kid I didn't know were working at the checkout counter. Hanging from the ceiling was Ms. Tanglemoth's list of library rules. No food. No drinks. No noise. No running. No nonsense. Rules that Ms. Tanglemoth made sure everyone followed.

Everything seemed normal in the library that day. But it wasn't.

As we walked past Ms. Tanglemoth, she barely glanced at us. That was strange. Usually, she swivelled her head to give every kid "the look." One of her eyes would narrow into a twitchy squint while the other grew round and large.

But today she kept her head down. Her narrow hands were doing a jittery dance with a pen. She could hardly hold still to write. Then she tilted her head in our direction and muttered, "Computers—surfing the Internet.

Aisle four. Bottom shelf at the end."

Duncan shot a blast of fear at me. Then he pulled me by my arm over to the huge wall of windows far away from Ms. Tanglemoth's desk. Sunlight warmed the row of tables and chairs, and only a few kids were rustling together at a distant table.

"I can't do this, Moon," he whispered feebly. "Did you hear what she said when we walked into the library? Ms. Tanglemoth told me where to find books about computers."

"So? Everyone knows you love computers."

"But I was thinking about my computer as we passed her—how I wish it was faster. Because I didn't want her to know what I was really thinking. Then she answered me as if I had spoken to her."

Duncan had planned to block his thoughts from Ms. Tanglemoth. I was impressed.

"Don't steam your brain cells, Duncan," I said. "She doesn't know anything yet." I too was scared that Ms. Tanglemoth would somehow guess my thoughts, but I wasn't about to let Duncan know that.

"She will soon enough." And his face turned the same white-green as his T-shirt.

Alarm bells rang inside my head, but I tried to silence them. "There are other kids here too. She can't possibly be listening to everyone at the same time. And we can close our minds to her. Besides, we're not doing anything wrong. We're just taking a look around."

"I don't know, Moon." Duncan had definitely come down with a bad case of nerves. I had to be strong enough for both of us.

I grabbed him by the shoulders and pulled his face down close to mine. "You promised me that you would help."

The kids at the nearby table stared at us. I had spoken too loudly.

"I know," Duncan agreed more softly. He shrugged himself free as the other kids turned back to their work. "But remember that I didn't hear any bells. And I don't have a new computer. And your mother hasn't appeared. You have no proof that anything magical has or will happen. And I just don't want to get into a hassle with Ms. Tanglemoth over something I can't see or hear."

I let out a sharp hiss of breath. "Look, Duncan. I don't know what I expect to find. I don't even know what to look for. And I know Ms. Tanglemoth isn't about to help me figure it out. I just want to snoop around. You be the lookout. Tell me if Ms. Tanglemoth is coming. She'll never suspect *you*."

Duncan made sure he never got in trouble at school. Teachers liked him, and kids liked him. Not like me. Everyone thought I was weird because of my short punky haircut and magic talk. Duncan didn't talk about magic to anyone but me.

"Okay, I'll back you up," he agreed with a deep sigh.

"Thanks," I said with relief. Then I quickly changed the subject before Duncan could change his mind. "Did you notice how weird Ms. Tanglemoth acted? She was definitely distracted by something. And she didn't even give us 'the look.'"

Duncan knew what I meant. "Yeah. It's weird. Maybe something strange is going on here." Then he tried to be helpful. "You should try to check out her back room."

"I thought about that. But how am I going to get in?"

Every kid in the school wondered what secrets Ms. Tanglemoth kept locked in her back room. But she never let anyone in, not even the caretakers. Kids dared each other to find out what was in there, but the door was always locked tight, and the keys jingled on a band around her wrist.

"Remember when Duff brought in a dead mouse?" I smiled. "He said that he'd found it in her back room." Duff is a bulky sports guy who has a great imagination.

"Yeah," said Duncan. "No one believed him. And he got sent to Principal Henry's office for bringing the mouse."

We shared a laugh. Then I said, "I bet she does magic back there."

"I bet she lives there. Hangs upside down to sleep," giggled Duncan.

"No," I continued wickedly, "she makes lizard-and-cockroach stew back there. But it's not her favourite. If she could only get her hands on a small child…"

Duncan's eyes grew wide and his hand flew to his lips. "Umm, Moon." He stared past my shoulder.

I felt a chill up my back.

"Moon Arlette," snapped Ms. Tanglemoth. "Did you come here to read or to chat?" She had caught us off guard, and I was sure she had heard my every word.

I froze at the sound of her voice. Wasn't Duncan supposed to be on the watch? But Duncan's legs were shaking so violently that he looked as if he were jogging on the spot.

I spun around. Ms. Tanglemoth's cold

eyes glared down at me over her pinched nose. Her grey hair was pulled back so hard from her face that her wrinkles were stretched unusually smooth.

Whenever I'm in a tight spot, a tiny voice talks to me from deep down in my guts. And if I shut up long enough and scrunch my brain until it hurts, I can hear what it says. Then I know what to do.

Just then, my little voice was talking, and I was listening. It told me I had to try to be fearless. I looked straight into Ms. Tanglemoth's grey-brown eyes and said, "Sorry about the noise. It won't happen again."

Ms. Tanglemoth peered at me as if she were trying to peek inside my mind, and I wanted to squirm away. Then she gave Duncan a long, searching look. I tried to lock my thoughts safely away from her, and I hoped that Duncan was doing the same. Without another glance at him, I grabbed a book off the nearest shelf and headed for the back of the library as if I were going somewhere important. I intended to circle around to Ms. Tanglemoth's desk. I hoped Duncan could keep her busy while I poked around. But I wasn't sure how long he'd manage it.

As I swung around the corner of the bookshelf to the back aisle of the library, the darkness hit me. No afternoon sunlight reached here. It was as gloomy as Ms. Tanglemoth's shadow. But, in spite of Ms. Tanglemoth, I loved that library. I liked the not-so-quiet sound of kids reading, the stale smell of the books and especially the books themselves. In those books, Duncan and I had read about all that magic could be—how to travel without leaving the room or wake up without an alarm clock. If only we could master what we'd read.

I moved along the back wall. Only an orange door broke the wall—the door to Ms. Tanglemoth's back room. Strangely, the door stood open a crack. I stopped still. My throat squeezed tight, my whole body trembled.

Was this a trick? Was Ms. Tanglemoth setting a trap for me? The idea raised mountains of goose bumps on my arms. She was sly enough to guess I was coming and to leave the door open. Or maybe it was just meant to happen? Maybe I was supposed to be here and the door was supposed to be unlocked for me? Maybe it was fate?

Either way, I had no choice. I had to go in.

"Just wait until Duncan hears about this,"

I thought to myself. I rubbed my arms to wipe away the goosebumps and forced my feet to slide forward. Feeling a little like a spy, I pushed the door gently and stepped in.

4

THE KEY

Ms. Tanglemoth's back room was dark and still. As if all the light and life had been sucked out of it. Even the light from the open doorway behind me could not shatter the blackness.

I held my breath, afraid that any sound would awaken some evil thing out of the darkness. Leaving the door ajar, I slid my hand along the cool brick wall to find the light switch. When my fingers finally touched the smooth plastic switch, I flicked it on. Fluorescent bulbs burst into life, and I dared to breathe again.

A twinge of excitement passed through me then. With eager eyes, I drank up the room. Mostly empty storage shelves crowded against one wall. Several cardboard boxes were stacked against the other.

"It's just a storage room," I thought with

disappointment. But I could see that Ms. Tanglemoth had made herself quite comfortable.

A low counter and a sink had been built under a wooden cupboard along the remaining wall. On the counter stood an electric kettle and some packages of tea. "So what! Ms. Tanglemoth drinks tea," I muttered. But somehow, I'd never imagined Ms. Tanglemoth eating or drinking anything—unless it was the blood of dead bats.

Beside the shelves stood a desk piled high with books, papers, and a photo of a black cat, inscribed "My dear Napoleon." And I'm not kidding when I say that the cat was black.

The thrill of getting into Ms. Tanglemoth's secret room paled quickly. The room was quite ordinary.

"What did you expect?" I asked myself. "A book of witches' spells and a cauldron?"

I opened a desk drawer and began riffling through the papers, pens and paperclips. "But there must be more than this," I said with a groan.

Then I saw a carved wooden box on the shelf above the desk. The shelf was decorated with potted artificial flowers and a few photographs—as if it was a special space for Ms. Tanglemoth. The box had been arranged in the centre of the display as if Ms. Tanglemoth had given it a place of honour.

"Now here's something," I thought. As I reached for the box, I accidentally knocked a stack of papers onto the floor.

Promising myself that I would pick up the papers before I left, I set the box on Ms. Tanglemoth's desk and then, feeling daring, I sat in Ms. Tanglemoth's chair.

The box was made from a reddish-brown wood that had been polished lovingly to a shine. A pattern of leaves had been carved along the top and sides. Curious, I opened the box. A royal-blue velvet cloth covered something lumpy. Cautiously, I unwrapped—a key!

An old-fashioned key lay on the velvet. It was a dull grey metal and the handle was shaped like a lacy spider web. I could feel the heaviness of the key through the rich velvet. It beckoned to me with its secrets—Ms. Tanglemoth's secrets.

The key was far different from the plain modern one that opened my apartment door. And it wasn't a key to any lock in the school—of that I was sure. I thought it must belong to some ancient, secret place. This key might open a chest filled with magic books, a gateway to the future, or a doorway to the centre of the universe. It held the promise of discovery. Overwhelmed by its mystery, I reached out to touch it.

As my fingers wrapped around it, a tingle ran through me, as if millions of tiny spiders were crawling over my skin, from my fingers to the very tips of my toes. I could feel my short hair bristle up with its touch, and my skin felt charged with a power beyond myself.

Startled, I tried to drop the key, but I couldn't release my grip. My body had stiffened and my muscles were tight wires. The key controlled me.

"Duncan!" I wanted to scream, but all I produced was a harsh, choking whimper.

My thoughts began to blur like puffs of smoky clouds. My body became limp and useless, and suddenly I couldn't see the desk, the box or the papers I'd scattered on the floor. My every sense had become focussed on a tiny speck of light deep in a dark place inside myself that I hadn't even known was there.

The soft spirit part of me pulled away from my body, tucked itself inside the light. I was drawn from Ms. Tanglemoth's back room into a dream that smelled and tasted real.

The sweet, strong smell of spring grass. The wild snort of a horse. A knight riding tall and straight. Chain mail, body armour and a grim look on his face. And a girl about my age on another smaller horse with a saddle trimmed in gold. Her hood pulled back. Long, deep-red hair hanging free over an apple-green cloak. Her face turned to catch the fresh breeze.

A castle stood proudly on a nearby hillside. The castle walls gleamed white, and red and blue flags waved from the towers. The early morning sunlight shone on the armour of the guards along the wall walk. The girl and the knight were heading toward this castle.

What was this place? Who were these people? Was this magic? Wonder and excitement flooded through me. I didn't want to do anything to break the spell. "Trust the magic," I thought to myself. I tried to relax and memorize every detail.

But the girl's face—I knew that face. Sky-blue eyes. Slender, pointed nose. Even the same tinkle of laughter like a song. Then I saw the sapphire-blue brooch that fastened her cloak. As big as a dollar coin, the sapphire dazzled against the white of her throat. It was just like the sapphire ring my mother had given me.

I felt strangely drawn to this girl—she looked like my mother. Suddenly, the wound opened again, and I felt the ache of the loss.

"Mom?" I thought, flooded with conflicting emotions. But at that moment, the key loosened its grip on me, and I let go.

I heard the thunk of the key as it hit the carpet and saw the carved box before me on the desk. Jumping backwards out of the chair in shock, I smashed my elbow against a bookshelf. Holding my elbow, I peered down at the key with a mixture of fear and wonder.

What had just happened? What had I seen? My head was still throbbing with images, feelings and smells. The musty sweat of the horses. The warmth of the sun. The red-haired girl with my mother's face.

Was I dreaming? Or was this Ms. Tanglemoth's magic—the secret she had tried to keep safe in her back room? Surely my wishing magic had led me to Ms. Tanglemoth to find this key. But who was this girl who looked so much like my mother? What did the key have to do with her or with Ms. Tanglemoth, or, for that matter, with me?

Suddenly, without even a moment to pull myself together, I heard the familiar sound of jangling keys. Ms. Tanglemoth. I froze like a raccoon caught in a flashlight's glare. Not only would Ms. Tanglemoth discover me in her back room, but she would find her papers in disarray and her magic key discovered.

How could I possibly explain?

5

ESCAPE

I jammed the box back up onto the shelf. Holding the velvet cloth in my hands, I snatched the key from the floor and shoved key and cloth into my pocket. Then I wedged myself between two wide storage shelves and lay flat against the floor. Papers still lay scattered everywhere, telling the story of my trespass. But I had no time to clean them up.

Ms. Tanglemoth poked her head through the open doorway. "Who's in here? What's going on?" she snapped sternly.

Then silence. All I could see was Ms. Tanglemoth's skinny ankles and her scuffed brown loafers. But I could imagine her eyes narrow and twitching as they scanned the room, her senses exploring like antennae. With her magic abilities, how could she not find me? I tried to make myself into a lifeless object.

No breathing. No thinking. I would melt into the faded brown carpet, and Ms. Tanglemoth would not notice me.

"Humph. Those kids are always making trouble," Ms. Tanglemoth muttered. Then I saw her hands picking up the mess of papers. "If I catch the brat who did this..."

Ms. Tanglemoth didn't finish her threat, but it was enough to set my heart thumping loudly. I was sure she would hear it.

I wished I could transport myself out of there. If wishing magic could get me into such a jam, why couldn't it get me out of it? A small part of me also wished that I'd gone straight home after school. Even my empty apartment would be better than this. But the immediate danger seemed to be over, and I wiggled forward to get a better look. Ms. Tanglemoth had stopped searching the room and was sorting the papers into neat piles. Her reading glasses swung from a chain around her neck, bumping softly about as she leaned over the desk.

As she arranged the papers, she continued to mutter. "Kids have no respect these days. How dare they enter my private office and toss papers like confetti! Oh, what are we going to do when these kids grow up, reckless and wild?" Ms. Tanglemoth was working herself into a state of despair.

Then she stopped in the middle of her rant. "But how did they get in? Did I forget to lock the door?"

She tilted her head up toward her carved wooden box high on the shelf over her desk. "Please, don't open it!" I wished silently.

But Ms. Tanglemoth only ran a trembling finger over the box. Then she withdrew her hand and said in a wobbly voice: "Oh, if only this hateful key were gone and done with! I must pull myself together."

My ears perked up when she mentioned the key, and I wanted to hear more. But what I heard was the click of the light switch, the bang of a door, and the sound of a key turning in the lock. Silence. I was locked in, in pitch darkness.

I lay still, afraid to make a sound. When my heart and breathing returned to normal, I began to worry. How was I going to get out? When would Ms. Tanglemoth come back? I couldn't let her find me with the key.

In a panic, I twisted my body out from behind the storage shelf and groped my way to the door. I tugged at the doorknob, but it was locked fast.

Then I felt it. Of course there had to be a way to unlock the door from the inside. I turned the handle and heard the bolt slide open. I was going to make it!

I slid out the door, shutting it with a soft click. When a voice spoke behind me, I jumped nervously.

"How did you get in there?" asked Duncan with amazement. He was speaking softly, but to me it sounded as if he were screaming in my ear.

"Duncan! Oh, I'm so glad it's you," I whispered, still shaking a little from the surprise. I glanced around, expecting Ms. Tanglemoth to be hiding behind a bookcase, just waiting for me. "We've got to get out of here, *now.*"

"You're afraid!" Duncan was surprised. "What happened?"

"Come on." I tugged at his arm.

"Okay, but I want to know what's going on." Duncan insisted.

I didn't have time for explanations. I just wanted to get safely away with the key. When Ms. Tanglemoth discovered the key was missing, I didn't want to be caught near the back room.

"The door was open, so I took a look," I

said quickly. "Then I got locked in. I have so much to tell you, but not right now. Let's just get out of here before she finds me out."

He let me drag him through rows of books. Just before we reached the big double library doors, I stopped abruptly.

"Stinking toenails," I whispered with frustration. "She's guarding the door."

Ms. Tanglemoth was standing behind her desk and glaring at each kid who passed by.

"So?" said Duncan. "We don't have anything to hide." Then he blurted a little too loudly, "By the way, if you were locked in, how did you get out?"

Ms. Tanglemoth's head snapped around, and her beady eyes focussed right on us.

I rammed my elbow into Duncan's ribs to get him to be quiet. "Quick, follow me," I hissed at him then raced past the librarian and out through the swinging doors.

"Moon and Duncan. No running in the library. Do you hear me? Come back here. I need to talk to you." Her voice carried through the doors.

We scurried around a corner, and I made a sudden turn into the boys' washroom, closely followed by Duncan.

"I'll hide here," I said. Who would ever

look for a girl in the boys' washroom? "You make sure she's not coming after us."

Duncan didn't comment on my great hiding place. "How am I supposed to do that without getting caught?" he whined.

He was right, losing Ms. Tanglemoth would be hard. She was craftier than a circus rip-off artist. But while I had the key, I had to keep out of her reach. "Try magic disappearing ink," I advised as I shoved him out the door. I was hoping that the washroom would stay empty.

The biggest surprise about the boys' washroom was that it was painted pink, just like the girls'. I would never have guessed that. But, to my surprise, someone was in one of the stalls, flushing. I quickly sneaked into another one and locked the door. I sat on the toilet and braced my feet against the stall door. I didn't want any company.

The pink walls around me were coloured and scratched with graffiti and I found myself reading the messages while I waited for Duncan. "Patrick loves Marta." "Duff is a dork." Then I saw one about me. "Moon is a witch." I smiled at that one.

But from my hiding spot, I couldn't help but hear the noises of the kid in the next stall, and I felt my cheeks burn with embarrassment. I didn't belong in there. I wanted to get out.

After waiting for what seemed like an eternity, I heard him leave the stall to wash his hands. When at last the washroom door thudded shut, I was more than relieved. I stood up and stretched my legs. The key, still wrapped in velvet in my pocket, weighed heavily on my mind. I had seen a castle when I touched it—and a girl with my mother's red hair and face. Then the vision had disappeared when I'd let go. I hadn't just imagined it, had I? I pulled out the key. Then I gently unwrapped it, careful not to touch it.

It lay unchanged, dull with age. I used the cloth to polish it, examining it closely. "What secrets do you hold?" I asked it. "What lock do you open?"

I wanted to touch the key—to feel the mysterious magic again. Just then someone pushed open the door to the boys' washroom. Hastily, I jumped back onto the toilet.

"Moon?" It was only Duncan, thank goodness.

I slid the key back into my pocket and stepped out from my hiding place in the stall.

"Don't you knock?" I joked.

"The coast is clear," he said. "A whole bunch of kids just went into the library.

She'll never leave them alone in there."

"Okay, let's go," I urged. "I'll tell you everything that happened once we get outside. And do I ever have a lot to tell," I promised. But I wasn't about to share any secrets until I was out of the boys' washroom and far away from Ms. Tanglemoth.

"No arguments from me," said Duncan. I think he'd had enough of Ms. Tanglemoth as well.

We raced down the hall toward the exit doors, keeping watch for Ms. Tanglemoth. As we shoved the doors open, a crisp wind cleared the dry school air from our lungs. I felt strong, even happy, as I jogged beside Duncan away from the school. The playground, the sidewalk, the houses and the trees flew by. We didn't slow down until we were around the corner from the school and far down the street toward our homes.

Duncan bent over, still breathing hard, with his hands on his knees. "Tell me about Ms. Tanglemoth's back room now, Moon," he gasped. Duncan was as curious about it as every other kid in the school.

"I have something to show you," I began proudly, taking in big gulps of air. "I found Ms. Tanglemoth's secret. And it has everything to do with my mother." I pulled the key out of my pocket to show Duncan, but it slipped out of the velvet and clattered onto the sidewalk right at his feet.

Duncan examined it closely.

"A key. A very old key. Is this the big secret?" he asked.

As he reached to pick it up, I gasped and grabbed his arm.

"No!" I screamed. "Don't touch it!"

6

PROOF

Duncan's hand halted in mid-air above the key. The wind that had been gently playing with the trees stopped too. I felt as if the whole world were holding still.

"Don't touch it," I repeated firmly, my voice shattering the stillness. A small red sports car zipped past us on the street. The wind began to tousle the leaves once more.

"I'm going to show you proof that magic is real," I said. "Proof that you can see. But I have something to tell you first." I couldn't let Duncan hold the key without warning, knowing what would happen. I wanted him to be prepared for his first true taste of magic.

"What are you talking about?" Duncan shook his head in confusion. But he stopped reaching for the key.

I scooped the key up into the velvet cloth. Then I pulled Duncan down to sit beside me on a shady piece of grass beside someone's hedge. We stretched our legs out across the sidewalk to gather the sun's warmth, and I told Duncan all about Ms. Tanglemoth's back room. How I had found the door open and discovered the box with the magical key on the shelf, and how Ms. Tanglemoth had almost caught me.

Duncan's eyes grew wider and wider until they seemed to fill his whole face. Then he interrupted, "You mean you stole Ms. Tanglemoth's key?"

I hadn't thought about it that way before. I'd just felt that I was meant to find the key. "Uh, well...I'll give it back." I stumbled over my words. "After we're finished with it."

I knew it was wrong to take the key, and that it looked as if I had stolen it. And really, I guess I had. But after I'd discovered its magic—and seen the girl—I just couldn't leave it there. In my mind, I was only borrowing it. I was sure I was meant to borrow it.

But Duncan wasn't impressed. "Moon!" he objected. "You can't keep the key."

"But just wait until I tell you everything else that happened."

Duncan frowned, but he listened to the rest of my story without any more interruptions. I told him how I'd seen a vision of an ancient castle when I touched the key, and of a girl who looked just like my mother. At that, he blinked and fixed his eyes on me with an unbelieving stare.

"Yeah, right, Moon." A skeptical grin crossed his face. "And my parents are alien space monsters."

He didn't believe me. I had told him the truth—offered to show him real magic—and Duncan didn't believe me.

I wondered if maybe he didn't want to believe me. Maybe he wasn't ready to believe in magic.

"Okay. There's only one way to prove it to you." I held the key out to him. "Touch it. Then you'll see."

"I will," he said stubbornly. And he reached out for the key.

Time slowed down for me as I watched Duncan's fingers approach the key. I wondered what he would see. The girl? The castle? The knight?

Then suddenly, I was jealous. Duncan would see the girl who resembled my mother while I watched him, unable to see anything. Or maybe he would have a different adventure, one that I couldn't share.

For a moment, I didn't want Duncan to touch the key. The magic was too delicious to share. I almost pulled the key away from him, but Duncan was, after all, my magic partner and my one true friend. He really understood why I wanted to believe in magic, why I had to believe in magic. Only Duncan realized that magic offered me hope—hope that I would have a happier life again. A life that included my mother. And I understood that a part of him wanted to find magic, too.

I held my hand out to him and stared into his nervous brown eyes. Then Duncan took a deep breath, wiped one hand clean on his jeans and grasped the key firmly.

I watched him carefully to see how the magic would take hold. I expected him to light up with the power of the key or shoot sparks from his fingertips.

But nothing happened.

Duncan turned to me and said, "I don't feel anything. There's nothing special about this old key."

"What did you do to it?" I accused him. "You destroyed the magic."

I wanted to grab the key out of his hand, to prove to myself that it still worked. At the same time, I was afraid to touch it. What if nothing happened? What if I had lost the only link to my mother? What if the magic was over before it had really begun? I couldn't wait to find out. I would prove to Duncan and myself that there was magic in this world. Magic enough to find my lost mother. I grabbed the key from him and braced myself for the shock.

Once again, I felt the tingling through my whole body. The strength of the key flowed around and through me until I thought it would lift me off the ground. I felt as if I might black out. I sensed Duncan edging away from me.

The stream of energy was strong—blurring my vision and making my head dizzy. I struggled against weakness, determined to keep control of myself and the key, until the light inside my head blinded me to the world around and my mind was swept into a magical place where my body could not travel.

A castle backed against steep cliffs above a wide river. Reeds on the river banks. Black birds gathered on small islands. Twin towers guarding the entrance to the castle gatehouse. Drawbridge lowered and iron grille raised in welcome. And far above the gatehouse, an enormous tower bragging that it could never be taken in battle.

I was relieved to see the same castle as before, but mostly I wanted to find the girl who looked like my mother.

Then I heard the knight's gruff voice. He spoke a language of long ago, filled with the expressions and syntax of an ancient tongue. Nevertheless, I understood every word.

"We will not arrive before morning mass. But soon you will be able to rest yourself, young Nora."

Nora. The girl's name was Nora. I was glad to know her name, but part of me was disappointed that her name was not Jane, like my mother's.

Then the girl spoke, her chin raised in defiance against the knight. "I could hardly be tired from the journey. This gift horse from Father has a sweet and gentle ride."

Her small horse did look fine, though it trailed the knight's charger. His huge horse stomped the earth with massive hooves, impatient with the slow pace.

"I don't mean to insult your palfrey, young

Nora," said the knight. "I'm only the messenger, sent from your father to protect you on this long journey home."

Nora relaxed her chin. "And you are true to this task, Madoc." Then she gazed at the castle with a dreamy smile. "I am glad to see the home of my childhood after so long an absence."

Madoc did not answer, but he too seemed eager to reach the castle. He urged his horse up the gentle slope of the hill, then over the drawbridge that spanned the moat in front of the castle. Nora and her horse followed his lead. Behind them trailed a wooden cart pulled by a plodding team of oxen.

As they crossed the drawbridge, Nora said happily, "I will share the laughter of my dear brother Edward once more, although I expect he is much changed since he became a knight."

"And delight to see your mother and father?" asked Madoc without much real interest. He seemed eager to be done with his escort duties.

A darker, worried look crossed Nora's face. "As the priest counsels, I shall honour my father and my mother."

They crossed into the shadow of the

gatehouse, and I suddenly felt awed by the strength of the castle's stone.

No torches were lit in the rounded passageway of the gatehouse, and the morning sunlight barely reached into its darkness. In the tunnel, clattering hooves echoed against stone. Noises from within the castle proved that many were already busy with the day's work.

Then I heard Nora speak once more, as if to herself. "I have learned all I need to know in my time away. Now it is time to prepare for my marriage. After twelve summers, my life as a noble lady is about to begin."

"Marriage?" I thought with surprise. Nora was the same age as me.

7

THE CASTLE

In the crowded courtyard, the sun was blinding. The deafening sounds of the animals, people, and crude machinery bounced off the castle walls. Wooden buildings housed animals, wagons and workshops. Two men were digging in a garden. And on a nearby wall walk, some guards stood sentry while others patrolled its length.

Then came the loud yapping of a rowdy pack of dogs.

"Move aside," yelled Madoc, his horse pushing Nora's off to the right. "Your father's leading a hunting party to the forest."

A large, fierce man led a crowd of hunters toward the gatehouse, the hunting dogs bounding ahead of them. Spotting Madoc and Nora, he gave them a brief nod of his head.

"Father!" called Nora, but he had already

entered the gatehouse passage.

Nora's face sagged with disappointment.

"He will be sure to greet you at dinner," said Madoc with a brief sideways glance at her.

"Indeed," agreed Nora, wiping all emotion from her face.

Across the courtyard stood another, smaller gatehouse. The second gatehouse led into an equally busy inner courtyard. The kitchen staff was building makeshift fireplaces in the courtyard. A commander was inspecting the castle guards, and a laundry woman was scrubbing clothes in a great tub. They passed the kitchen and sleeping quarters. Madoc halted his horse and dismounted.

"It was my pleasure to serve you on this journey." He bowed awkwardly to Nora. "Now, I will see your palfrey to the stables."

"Thank you, Madoc," answered Nora as she jumped down. "I'm eager to climb the stairs to the Great Tower once again. I hope to find Mother and Edward."

As Madoc led away the horses, Nora headed toward the largest tower in the castle.

"I can see why they call this the Great Tower," I thought.

The Great Tower was three stories high,

with the entrance into a great hall on the second level. Huge wall hangings showed colourful scenes—the castle being built, the hunting of deer in the forest and a girl in a garden. The walls were decorated in a design of gold and green triangles and diamonds. From the floor of the great hall, two spiral staircases led to an open gallery along one end of the tower, where the windows let in slivers of dusty sunlight.

The great hall was no quieter than the courtyard. Servants rushed about carrying pots, bringing in rushes for the floors and hanging fresh-smelling herbs in bundles on the walls. More servants vied for the attention of one man who was the centre of all this hubbub.

Then a young knight hailed Nora from the gallery above the great hall.

"Nora!"

People were beginning to cluster around Nora like bees, but she brushed them off.

"Edward!" She rushed up the curved stone stairway to greet him.

As they met and hugged, I couldn't help noticing how alike they were. Almost like twins. Tousled satin red hair and deep blue eyes. Edward a head taller in brightly-coloured clothing, and Nora slighter in a flowing gown.

After they had greeted each other, they whispered together as they watched the bustle in the great hall below.

"The lord of the castle must keep up his position. But, my sister, there has been talk. Our father is not beloved by the common folk. I fear trouble," said Edward in a hushed voice.

"What do you mean, Edward?" Nora's pale face wrinkled with worry.

Edward continued. "There has been talk of Father's cruel treatment of both servants and peasants. He demands their crops, even their seed corn. His deeds are brutal in the heat of battle. He feasts while the peasants go hungry. Some among us are not happy. I don't want to frighten you, Nora, but you must take care to always please him. His temper has worsened. Even Mother cannot keep the peace."

Nodding her head, Nora pulled her cloak tighter around her. "Do not fear for my safety. I shall soon be married and living far away with my husband."

"Yes, Father speaks with great impatience of your wedding. He is sure that your marriage will improve his political fortunes."

"I am but a pawn in Father's game of chess," sighed Nora.

"We will protect your interests, dearest sister," promised Edward. "You can be sure of my word. Now, let us go tell Mother that you are home."

As Nora and Edward turned away, I wanted to follow them to meet their mother. But something pulled me back into my world. The key had released me once more.

As my head began to clear, I could see the green leaves above me and feel the hard sidewalk under my legs. The images of the castle still haunted me. Nora's world lingered in my thoughts. I was peaceful there—as if the key were guiding me toward my mother. I longed to understand the ties between Nora and me.

"Moon? Are you okay?" asked a voice.

I nodded.

Duncan. I wanted to tell him what I'd seen. The magic still worked—it just hadn't worked for him. But he was too busy firing questions at me.

"What happened? What's going on, Moon? You stiffened up as if you were in a trance or something. It really gave me the creeps." Duncan was standing back from me as if he feared he would catch some deadly disease.

"Sit down." I patted the grass beside me, then I told him everything I had seen.

"The magic is real," I said finally.

"Maybe," he shrugged. I sensed that Duncan still didn't really believe me.

"How much proof do you need?" I wanted to ask, but I didn't want to argue with him.

"But we still shouldn't keep the key," he persisted.

I ignored him, changing the topic. "I've read about this kind of magic. How some people can see the past by holding an object in their hands. It's as if the object can somehow send memories connected to it, and people can receive them."

"Kind of like a highway into the past," added Duncan.

"Yeah." I was glad that he was getting interested now. Although I felt special because the magic had worked for me, I still wanted Duncan to share my excitement.

"Try touching it again," I urged him.

He did. Duncan passed the key from hand to hand repeatedly, but it was no use. His wires were crossed, his stars weren't in harmony, his highway to the past just didn't lead anywhere.

"Why does the key work for me but not for you?" The question bothered me.

"I don't know." Duncan fingered the key again.

Then I had a thought. Maybe Duncan couldn't see Nora or the castle because he didn't really believe in magic. Or maybe he hadn't tapped into the magical part of himself. But I didn't say that to Duncan.

"Do you think it works for Ms. Tanglemoth?" I asked instead.

"Probably," he answered. "After all, she kept it as if it were something really special."

Finally, Duncan passed the key back to me. "We'll talk tomorrow, Moon. I told my mother I'd be home for an early supper."

As I shoved it back into my pocket, the excitement of the day began to melt from me. Home. What was there at home to look forward to?

"I'd better get home too," I agreed, as a deep loneliness replaced the excitement inside me.

We headed down the street together toward the corner where Duncan would turn left and I would turn right. Duncan to his family-filled house, me to my empty apartment. Waiting until my father finally slouched through the door after work. The usual routine of eating supper while he watched the news on TV. And the sadness of missing my mother.

8

EMPTY

The drone of the news on television echoed through the empty space that my mother used to fill. My father let the noise wash over him. Even when shouting angry people blasted across the screen and startled me, he paid little attention to anything but his supper.

We ate in front of the TV every night. I think it was Dad's excuse not to talk. He hardly ever spoke to me any more, and he would never answer my questions about Mom or where she might be. It's as if he'd got stalled when she left and couldn't get started again.

Beside him on the faded couch, I leaned over the coffee table and pushed my food around on my plate. The smell of burnt toast and boring pasta-from-a-box didn't excite my tastebuds. And, unlike my father,

I wasn't trying to forget Mom, but to remember.

Every night I played a game with myself. I plugged my ears to block the sound of the TV, then squinted my eyes to distort the room. If I worked it right, I could imagine the house we had rented before my mother left. And I pretended the three of us were together and happy again.

But that night I just couldn't make it work. I couldn't erase the beige walls, the jagged crack on the ceiling or the voices of the neighbours in the apartment hallway. My mind was all jumbled up with thoughts of my mother, the key and Nora. I needed to talk to someone who understood me.

Looking at Dad, I wondered, "Could I talk to him about the castle girl?"

I searched his face for an answer. Plain and sad with the shadow of a beard. Chocolate-coloured hair matching mine. Grey eyes too dull to catch the light. White dress shirt hanging loose over navy pants. His tie crumpled on the worn brown rug. Thin body with a bulge around his middle.

Then, with a long groan, Dad lifted his feet onto the coffee table, his knees cracking and popping with the effort. Leaning back into the couch, his arms folded over his rounded stomach, he settled himself in for the night.

"I can never explain the magic key to him," I thought with a sigh. "It would be like talking Martian to him. He wouldn't understand."

I picked up my father's empty plate and my own full one and carried them to the kitchen. Each night, my father made the supper, and I cleaned up. That was the deal. Sometimes I bellyached about it, but that night I didn't mind doing the dishes. It gave me time to think and to get away from the endless droning of the TV—the TV that my father never turned off. I dumped the dishes and ran the water in the sink. First the plates and cups, then the cutlery and finally the sticky pot.

While I washed up, I thought, not for the first time, about how to contact my mother. Would Nora somehow lead me to her? We were hardly in the same time-frame. I wondered where Mom might have gone. Where was she now? Was she living here in the same city that I was? I imagined her in a crummy apartment eating dinner by herself. Or had she found new friends, maybe a new family? The idea terrified me.

Even though my father refused to talk about her, I decided to ask him again about Mom. I needed some answers. Rushing through the rest of the dishes, I propped the pot to drip-dry in the dish rack and headed back to the living room.

The news was over, and Dad was flipping channels. He settled on a game show as I dropped onto the couch beside him. The host of the show was introducing the three contestants, but I didn't care, nor, from the blank look on his face, did Dad.

"I was just wondering, Dad," I started, "did you, um, ever hear anything from Mom? Like where she was, or something?"

The words hung in the air between us. I wondered if he had even heard me. He still did not respond.

Then, just as I was about to launch another question, he shifted his weight on the couch and brought his legs down to the floor.

I took it as a signal of his attention. "I just thought that, once she got settled, she might have called or written. And maybe you forgot to tell me."

The answer was slow in coming. "Nope," he said simply. "No letters. No phone calls." I was glad to hear him speak, but we had gotten this far before. He would admit to not hearing from her. After that, he wouldn't say anything more.

But this time, I was going to push him harder. "Well, do you think she might be staying with a friend or someone from her family?"

I had often wondered about my mother's family, because we had never, ever gone to visit them. My mother would never talk about them. I knew some of their names, and that they lived in a smaller, nearby city, but, for some reason, we had been cut off from them, cut out of their lives. If Mom were with them, I had no way of finding out.

Dad only shook his head slowly, without taking his eyes off the TV. He said nothing.

"Dad!" I yelled louder than the TV, jumping up to stand between him and it. "Do you know anyone we can call who might know where she is?"

My father's voice was low and sad, but he did glance up from the screen. "I called everyone already, Moon."

A hint. A lead. A clue. Maybe a letter from her. That was all I wanted. Was that too much to hope for?

Tears suddenly rushed to my eyes, but I

blinked them back. "Would you even tell me if she did phone?" I confronted my father.

"Moon..." Dad started to say.

The TV audience exploded with cheers and clapping, and Dad's eyes flashed back to it. But I wasn't finished with Dad yet. With the smack of a button, I turned off the TV.

"Maybe it's your fault that she left." My voice was high and cracking. "What did you do to drive her away?"

Before he could reply, I dashed down the hall to my room. When the TV came on again, I felt lonelier than before. I knew that he wouldn't follow me.

I flopped down on the striped Mexican blanket covering my bed and wiped madly at my tears. When my eyes finally cleared, I stared furiously at the photos of my mother that covered the walls, and I wished for the zillionth time that she would call or write.

Then another idea struck me. The reason I could use the magic of the key and Duncan couldn't—maybe the key had more to do with my mother than I knew. Maybe the key was a clue to finding her. Was that why I could see Nora and Duncan couldn't? Had Mom left a way to seek her out, wherever she was?

I pulled the cloth-wrapped key from my pocket and held it in my palm. If the key led to my mother, I wasn't going to wait a moment longer to use it.

As my fingers touched the key itself, the familiar burst of energy shot through me. My body felt as if millions of fireflies were tickling my insides. I grabbed the blanket in my free hand and squeezed, forcing myself not to yell out. Holding on tightly, I waited first for the darkness, then the light that would transport me to Nora's castle.

9

THE FEAST

Noon-day sun in a cloudless sky. A horn sounding loudly. People in plain clothing mixing with others in rich, colourful robes climbing the stairs to the Great Tower.

Something important was happening. In the hall of the Great Tower, benches stretched out beside tables that were spread with white tablecloths and set with knives, spoons, cups and shallow wooden bowls. Thick slices of bread lay like plates at each place. Hundreds of candles flickered and smoked from large iron rings suspended from the ceiling. More candles were supported in wall brackets and on tall candlesticks, but even so, the hall was dim compared to the bright sun outside.

Musicians in the gallery above prepared their instruments. People jostled for seats at the many tables. Near the only fireplace, a long table stood importantly on a raised platform. There sat Nora with her brother Edward, her father, a woman I guessed was her mother and a few others. At a nearby table, I noticed Madoc laughing with a group of knights.

Nora's father and mother sat regally on massive chairs, ready to drink from silver cups and to eat from silver-rimmed bowls with silver spoons. Nora and her mother were talking quietly together, both dressed in long silk cloaks and elegant gowns. Nora's mother wore an elaborate head covering, her veil thrown back to show a face much like my mother's. Nora's hair, hanging loose to her waist, was encircled by a garland of flowers. The sapphire brooch at her neck once again brought me a rush of happy memories about my mother.

After a man in heavy robes stood to say grace, servants with jugs, basins and towels rushed to help everyone wash their hands. Bread and drinks were served with great ceremony. Then trumpets and drums announced the entrance of the first dish.

I couldn't begin to describe the huge quantities of food that emerged from the kitchen. I made out peacock, meat pies, boar's heads, salmon, seafood, fish custard and stew. Then came sweet pies and even birds cooked in pies. Two whole oxen had been roasted in the courtyard, which made me remember uneasily the oxen that had pulled Nora's cart home. After several courses had been served, I was amazed when the servers brought out even more food. There were fruits, nuts, cheese, wafers and more drink. So much food that the spices tickled the air.

The guests' manners left a lot to be desired. They chewed, spat and belched their way through the feast. They talked loudly, and a fight erupted between Madoc and another knight. The chaos almost made me appreciate my own wordless dinners with my father.

Nora's father tossed a large hunk of meat to one of the hunting dogs that scuttled beneath his feet. The dogs looked better fed than some of the servants.

Nora's father wore a dazzling outfit of purple and gold. Jewels sparkled from his rings and belt. Brightly coloured stockings covered his legs and long, pointed shoes graced his feet. A close-fitting white cap covered his hair and ears and tied under his chin. His beard and moustache were short.

With a grin that was almost pleasant, he began to speak to Edward beside him. "Look upon these people for what they can give you. The peasants are only worth as much as their labours and taxes, the knights for their courage in battle."

Nora's mother was sitting beside them, with Nora beside her. From where they sat, they couldn't help but hear Nora's father speak.

"Such talk!" Nora's mother tried to hush him by heaping more meat on his plate.

The lord glared at his wife, his face mirroring his bad temper. "And a wife is only worth the wealth gained through marriage," he announced loudly to Edward.

Edward was silent, and Nora's mother pretended not to hear. Nora looked miserably down at her plate.

"Even the king's favour is only a means to increase your might," scowled Nora's father. "Live for the land, Edward. Land is all that matters, for it will give you what you need. Land is power." He gave a broad sweep of his hand and laughed.

"Yes, Father," Edward replied dutifully. Not until the tables were cleared did Nora's father address the crowd. The leftovers had been gathered for the poor. The servants had repeated their hand-washing duties. When Nora's father raised his massive frame from his chair and held out his hands, silence fell across the hall.

His voice boomed off the walls and flew up to the high ceiling as he directed attention to Nora. "With this feast, we welcome my daughter home."

Cries and cheers erupted, but he silenced them. "And yet, all too soon she will leave us."

The guests waited, not sure how to react.

"Ah, but do not despair," he continued, "for in a fortnight, my daughter will be wed to Gilbert, first-born son of Balich." He thumped his huge hands on the table. The people followed his lead.

"We know the man Balich as a mighty warrior and master of vast tracks of fertile land. His son, Gilbert, heir to all, is bound to prove himself just as worthy. Promised to each other as children, they have not met since the betrothal ceremony. Gilbert, I give you my daughter."

Then a boy not much older than me stood up. He too was sitting at the main table, but at the far end. His fine tunic hung loose over his chest, and his face was so pale and sunken that I knew he was ill. Gilbert nodded quickly to the crowd and to Nora then sat down.

Nora's father let the crowd cheer wildly for a moment. He whispered to Edward, "And we shall expand our territory to include that of Nora's young husband." Then he roared to the crowd. "Together, we drink to their wealth, happiness and godliness in the years ahead."

The guests yelled good wishes toward Nora and Gilbert.

But in spite of the calls of the crowd, Nora remained still, staring at the faces around her, a shadow of a frown above her unhappy eyes. "Am I to marry a man who looks so close to death? Is that why we are to be wed sooner than expected?" she asked aloud.

"Shh." Nora's mother silenced her. "Ours is not always a world of choice."

Then Nora glanced at Edward, who was smiling at her with sad, glistening eyes. Finally, she managed to offer him a weak smile in return.

My stiff fingers uncurled to release the key, and my mind began to shake free of the castle vision. I gazed sleepily around my room as if I had just woken from a dream, not sure for a moment where I was.

Then I lay still on my bed, trying to sort through what I'd seen. Nora's mouth, so like my mother's, her father's wicked grin, the scent of the spiced food in the air and the slurps and gossip of the crowd as they ate.

The key lay beside me on the bed—only a touch away from my fingertips. I could clasp it again if I wanted to, returning to Nora's world for a link to my mother.

But the trip had exhausted me. The next magic journey would have to wait. I found enough energy to wrap the key and shove it under my mattress. Then I fell back onto the bed, still in my T-shirt and jeans, ready for sleep.

10

HUNTED

I awoke with fresh hope that I would somehow puzzle out the meaning of my adventures in Nora's world. I just knew that, maybe not that day, but soon, Nora would give me a clue. And I had a plan.

Jumping out of bed, I dumped yesterday's clothes—all wrinkled from sleep—on the floor and rummaged through my drawers for something clean.

"Nora's castle might exist somewhere in the real world," I thought. "I just have to try to find it. Maybe I will learn more about Nora. Maybe I'll discover the lock that fits the key, and why that key is important."

The clock showed that I was running late. Quickly I pulled on a red T-shirt and blue jeans.

Then it struck me—I couldn't research castles in the school library. Ms. Tanglemoth would be there. She probably knew by now that I had her key. Wouldn't she demand it back? I imagined myself innocently reading a castle book while Ms. Tanglemoth circled me like a lioness circles her prey.

I shivered. Was Ms. Tanglemoth really a witch? I felt hunted. No way could I go to the library as long as Ms. Tanglemoth was laying traps for me. I would have to find a way to avoid her all day long at school. If I made it through the day without her catching up with me, I could head to the community library with Duncan.

"Well, whatever happens," I said to myself, "I am not going to give up the key." I slid a hand under my mattress until my fingers brushed against the velvet cloth, just for reassurance.

Glancing into the mirror, I smoothed a hand over my hair—it was too short to need a comb. Next I hurried to the bathroom to clean my teeth. I could hear my father banging around the kitchen.

"Breakfast, Moon," he called to me.

As I barely wiped the toothbrush over my teeth, Dad called me again.

"Did you hear me? Hurry up or I'll be late for work."

I scanned the schoolyard for Duncan. I wanted to tell him about the latest castle vision. But he wasn't in the pack of kids who were gathered near the school doors. I checked out the kids collecting along the sidewalk and sauntering past the huge old trees that grew along the far edge of the baseball diamond, but Duncan was nowhere in sight.

I wanted to avoid any possible meeting with Ms. Tanglemoth, so I crouched against the rough trunk of an old maple tree, near a side entrance to the school. Not that I had ever seen Ms. Tanglemoth in the schoolyard before. But just maybe, if she wanted me badly enough, she might venture out.

Ten minutes before the bell, there was still no sign of Duncan. I passed the time staring down at a caterpillar crawling up a tall blade of grass. Then Duncan's familiar black-and-white sneakers appeared on either side of the caterpillar.

"Hey, Moon," he said.

"Duncan! We've got to talk." I leaped up beside him. I told him I'd used the key again the night before. I described everything—

Nora at the feast, her father's speech, her sadness and even the food that the guests had eaten.

Duncan's eyebrows shot up as he swept the hair from his eyes. His forehead knotted into a huge question mark. "I'm beginning to think this castle may be real, Moon. Not even you could make all that up."

"Great," I said, pleased that he was starting to believe me. "Then you'll come with me to the community library after school to read up on castles? I want to find the one that was Nora's castle."

"I have a better idea," he countered, flushing with enthusiasm. "Let's go to my house after school. We can do an online computer search for castles."

"Okay," I agreed. "If that castle is real, we'll find it. But don't get too excited yet. We still have a problem. A big problem."

"What?" Duncan looked worried.

"How are we going to stay out of Ms. Tanglemoth's way? By now, she must have discovered that her key is missing, and I bet we're her first suspects."

"I've been thinking about that." Duncan sighed. "But we can't avoid her if she wants to corner us. She could call our parents. Or come into one of our classes. She could even use her magic against us." Duncan's rounded shoulders trembled.

I felt myself shudder. "Well, we know for sure she's going to be looking for us. What can we do?"

"Well, it is her key," Duncan said. "Maybe you should give it back to her."

I glared. "No way, Duncan. Forget it. That key has something to do with my family—Nora looks just like my mother. Our wishing magic led me to the key. I've got to find out why that key came to me."

Duncan's eyes grew a little wider, but he didn't say anything right away. Then he spoke softly, "Or maybe you're making up reasons why you don't have to give the key back."

Anger bubbled up inside me. Didn't he get it? The key was important in my life.

The buzz of the school bell interrupted us, although I could hardly call it a bell. Our school had a modern buzzer that sounded more like a super-large insect flying overhead.

Duncan and I looked at each other nervously. We still faced the same problem. How were we going to avoid Ms. Tanglemoth all day long?

"Maybe we could transfer to a new school," I suggested. And I didn't mean it as a joke.

"What are we going to do?" Duncan's eyes flashed anxiously.

"Just lie low. And stay away from the library." I tried to sound calm.

Then there was nothing to do but fall in line behind the other kids.

We filed through the door and down the hall toward our lockers. Although I was watching for her, I didn't see Ms. Tanglemoth marching down the hall until it was too late.

My heart flip-flopped in my chest. Duncan was so terrified that he hid behind me, which was pretty funny when you consider that he is taller than I am. His quick, sharp breaths raised hairs like prickles on the back of my neck. Then the kids we were following stopped at their lockers and we were left unprotected, exposed. Fresh meat ready to be eaten by Ms. Tanglemoth.

I tried to swallow my fear—to act cool. Was I ever glad that I had left the key at home. But Duncan was walking so closely behind me that he stepped on the back of my shoes.

"Duncan," I hissed out of the corner of my mouth, "get off my shoes."

But Duncan wouldn't budge from his safe spot. Then he really tripped me up. He leaned into me and since I couldn't move my feet, I ended up sprawled on the floor right in front of Ms. Tanglemoth. And Duncan was left standing on my shoes, face to face with her.

To our amazement, she hardly glanced at us. Her eyes darted about, looking everywhere but at us. She seemed to be avoiding us as much as we wanted to avoid her.

She wasn't hunting us. If someone had tripped in front of her at any other time, I would have expected a lecture about keeping in your own space—three strides behind the person in front of you. But she didn't even lecture us.

With her nose pointed toward the ceiling tiles, she stepped carefully over my legs. At the last second, just when I was sure that she was going to march down the hallway away from us, she reached out a hand to help me up.

"Uh, thanks, Ms. Tanglemoth," I said without looking at her eyes. I felt a twinge of guilt for taking her key.

As she released my arm, she whispered angrily, "Have you no respect? Did you have to disturb my papers? Well, maybe you'll have better luck with that bothersome key."

Then she left Duncan and me staring after her in surprise.

"Can you believe that?" I asked him. "She must have figured out by now that I took the key, and she's letting me keep it. But why? Doesn't she want it back?"

"I just don't get it," replied Duncan.

11

THE SEARCH

Ms. Tanglemoth continued to ignore us for the rest of the day. We couldn't figure out what she was up to. All the same, I was glad when school was over and we headed toward Duncan's house.

In our neighbourhood of small houses, Duncan's definitely stood out. Whenever I went there, I always compared it to my tiny apartment. The house was enormous—the biggest on the street. The lawn was a cushy carpet edged with perfect round bushes and tall spiky trees. And inside always smelled good—like vanilla ice cream.

I perched on a tall swivel-stool in the kitchen and spun around in circles. Duncan poured some lemonade and put some cookies on a plate. His cat, Puddles, wound around my chair, purring up at me.

"That you, Duncan?" called a voice from

the next-door den. Duncan's mother worked from home. She was a software programmer, and his Dad ran a restaurant downtown.

"Yeah, Mom," answered Duncan. "I'm here with Moon. We're just getting some snacks and then we're going to my room."

"Okay, dear. I'm just finishing up. Don't forget, we're going downtown to meet your father for dinner tonight."

"Yeah," called Duncan. "I won't forget."

With the cookies and lemonade, we climbed the wide spiral staircase to the second floor. Duncan's room was massive, with a double bed, two dressers, an L-shaped desk and shelves of computer programs, games and books. His desk was huge too, and you could tell that he spent a lot of time there because it was scattered with disks, CDs, bits of paper and a plate with a few leftover crumbs.

"Have a cookie," offered Duncan. "My father made them." He held out the china plate with soft pink flowers around the edge.

"Thanks." I wondered if my Dad would ever bake me homemade cookies.

As I bit into the cookie, hunks of chocolate and nuts in a chewy sweetness melted in my mouth. I quickly finished the cookie and reached for a second one.

"I'll just start up my computer," Duncan said.

"What's going on in here?" asked someone else. Then a head with the same straight dark hair as Duncan's popped around the doorframe. It was Kirk, Duncan's annoying older brother. I said before that Duncan's family was just about perfect. And it was—except for Kirk.

"Get lost, Kirk," snapped Duncan. He stared at the computer screen as if his brother weren't even there.

Kirk was dressed in a baseball uniform. When he saw me, he smirked. "Oh, your girlfriend's here again."

Kirk was always bugging us like that. I guess he thought that we weren't supposed to hang out together. After all, most girls my age only hung out with other girls and the guys only hung out with other guys. It's an unwritten rule that Duncan and I chose to ignore.

But Duncan was fuming at his brother. "Butt out," he ordered him.

Then I added, "We're studying, baseball brain." Kirk didn't care about anything but baseball.

"Yeah, right," said Kirk slyly, but he left.

Duncan was furious. "He's been an even bigger jerk since his coach told him he has a chance at making the pros."

I nodded. I was pretty sick of Kirk's stupid comments too.

"Okay. Computer's ready," he said, his voice suddenly sounding happier. "Let's see what we can find out about castles."

I pulled a chair over beside him, near the computer, and peered at the screen. "I'll start," I directed.

An hour later, the cookies were gone, but the search was just beginning. We still hadn't found the castle. "I thought this would be easier," I sighed.

"I know," answered Duncan. "There's just so much stuff on castles."

"But I thought we'd have found it by now."

"Me too," he agreed. "But don't worry. We'll find it. It'll just take some time, that's all."

"We've found everything about castles except what we want to find." And we had.

We'd found a company named Castleguard that made computer software. We'd found a chat group called Castletown that seemed to talk about everything but castles. We'd found a castle that was now a hotel. Most of the information was aimed at people who wanted to travel. We'd found castles turned into restaurants, hospitals and sports centres. We'd even found a list of castles for sale.

All the castles we'd found were more like huge homes than the fortress-like castle we were looking for. These places had drawing rooms and libraries. They had paintings of their owners. They were definitely not Nora's castle.

"These places are not right at all," I said with frustration.

"Wait. Look at this!" Duncan had found a company that provided research on castles—for a fee. It offered information about castles that were open for visitors. And it helped people find certain castles or types of castles.

"We could get them to find the castle for us," I said, thrilled that we'd finally found something.

"But where are we going to get the money?" asked Duncan. "They don't do it for free, you know. And besides, what are we going to tell them about the castle? We don't know its name, or where it is. We know nothing except what it looks like. How would we describe it to them?"

I refused to admit defeat. "I could draw it," I explained. "I've walked through most of the castle. Then we could send the drawing to this company and ask them to research it for free because we're kids. They might go for it. You never know."

"Yeah, I guess so." Duncan wasn't convinced. "Let's just look around a bit more and see what else we can find first."

And we did find better information. For another hour, we read about building castles, life in a medieval castle and castle defences. We watched video tours of castles. We found photos, maps and floor plans of castles around the world.

"There are so many castles. I never realized..." I started. Then I lost myself in the legends of another castle.

"It's pretty neat," answered Duncan. "Hey, did you read that no siege was ever successful on this castle?" He pointed to the screen. "One army waited four months for the defenders to surrender, but they never did. And the attackers couldn't break down the castle defences. Cool."

"Yeah. And historians think this castle dates back to the times of King Arthur and the Knights of the Round Table."

"I would've made a great knight," bragged Duncan.

"Oh, really," I laughed. "The knights looked tough to me. They might have chopped you up into little bits."

"What do you know?" But my teasing didn't bother Duncan. He was enjoying himself.

We continued scanning the castles until Duncan said excitedly, "Look at this one. Maybe it's the one."

But I just glanced at it and shook my head. "That's the third time you've said that. It's all wrong. There shouldn't be a tower there, and the gatehouse is too small."

Duncan fell silent, then he said quietly, "Remember, Moon, I haven't seen the castle. Only you have."

I felt sorry then—sorry for Duncan. I could remember how desperately I wanted to work magic. How much I still wanted to believe that magic could turn my life around. I hoped that Duncan could work magic too someday.

Just then, Duncan's mother interrupted us. Dressed in jeans and a sweatshirt, she bounced cheerfully into the room. "Come on, Duncan. It's time to go." Then she noticed me. "Hi, Moon. You'd better get going too. Your father will be wondering where you are."

I checked my watch. Dad would have arrived home half an hour ago. I quickly packed my bag to leave, but Duncan made no move to get up. He was searching yet another site for the castle.

"Really, Duncan," said his mother. "What's so interesting?"

Duncan barely glanced up. "We're just working on a project."

"Well, you can finish it tomorrow then," insisted his mother. "Let's go. Your father will be waiting for us at the restaurant."

"Okay, just a minute." Duncan loved eating at his Dad's restaurant. Until then, I'd never seen him reluctant to go.

"We'll work on this tomorrow, right, Moon?"

"I'm free," I said casually. I liked seeing Duncan so eager.

"Right after school?" he asked.

"I'll be there." I headed downstairs to let myself out.

12
THE WAR COUNCIL

Where have you been? Do you know what time it is?"

Dad barked out the questions as soon as I opened the door. Hands on his hips, his brows knotted together, he blocked the narrow hallway.

I bent over and pretended to struggle with a knot in my shoelace. Why was Dad so upset? He hadn't paid me this much attention in months. Right then, I wanted to get to my room, to find the castle key hidden under my mattress and to escape to Nora's world once more. But he was yelling at me and blocking my way.

"I was at Duncan's. Sorry," I muttered. Dad took it for granted I'd be home first, waiting for him to finish work. He didn't know what it was like to wait.

"Why were you late? Why didn't you call?"

His voicc rose steadily, almost to a scream.

"Leave me alone!" I shouted back at him. "You're always late, so why are you yelling at me?"

I pushed past his dark shape and ran down the hall. Past the kitchen, where microwaved trays of chicken and vegetables lay ready on the counter. But I didn't care about food.

With relief, I slammed the door to my room behind me and listened carefully for the fallout. No footsteps. Nothing. Just the tin-can sound of voices from the TV. Had Dad given up on the whole argument? He was probably settling himself in front of the TV for the night.

Jamming my arm under the mattress, I reached until I felt the cool touch of the velvet bundle. As I pulled the key out from its hiding spot, I remembered the questions that still plagued Duncan and me. We hadn't found the castle. Or much else, either.

But I was eager to feel the familiar tingle of power from the key. I wanted to be swallowed whole by another castle vision. As I grabbed hold of the key, its energy surged through my body and overwhelmed me once again with its strength. Thoughts of my father melted into a dark fog, swirling in confusing circles with the key's power. Then my mind filled with the light of another castle dream.

A narrow shaft of evening light cut across the gloom inside the Great Tower. A few candles burned below in the great hall, where servants bustled back and forth, arranging straw mattresses on the floor.

Nora huddled in the gallery against the wooden railing, peeking down at the scene in the great hall below. She focussed on her father, Edward, and a circle of knights. They were discussing a message sent to them from their long-time enemies.

"The scoundrels dare to band together against me?" exploded Nora's father. At the sound of his voice, the servants fled the room. The knights remained behind.

Nora's father, dressed in elaborate robes with a white cap, paced violently around the others.

"No noble blood flows through their bodies. I will swat them like flies," he continued. Then he tore the message from the hands of one of the knights and read it again with terrible concentration.

"My lord," began one knight humbly. His robes were also lavish, but he was not wearing a white cap. "If I may be so bold as to speak? With three lords united in one force...well, that is thrice the number of men—thrice the fighting force. Their troops would greatly outnumber our own."

Nora's father didn't hear the knight's words. He was reading the message. "They call my attacks on their lands ignoble. They accuse me of overreaching ambition and brutality. They say I have no rightful claim to the land I took from them—that I should simply return it." He paused to throw back his head and roar with laughter—a fierce, threatening laughter. His eyes were pits of blackness.

"I curse them and their children," he snarled. "I curse their lands and their wives. I shall destroy everything they own. To battle, men. A glorious conquest awaits. Together we shall plunder their lands until we beat them into the fools that they are. Then you shall have your prize. I promise a gift of land to each and every one of you."

"My lord," began the knight again, "that this is a message of war—of that we are all certain. And to meet their demands—to return the lands we have won from them—that is unthinkable. But we have had word that, without awaiting your reply, our enemies are already gathering for an attack on your lands and this very castle. They are already laying waste to the countryside and destroying all who oppose them."

"I fear them not," roared Nora's father. "I welcome the thrill of battle, as should all my knights. Of late, I have seen too many quarrels among our own. Training and patrols are not enough for fighting men. We shall unleash our forces in battle against our enemies."

When the council knights began to cheer loudly, Nora's father gestured for silence. "As you know, the King himself granted these lands and this castle to me for service to the Crown. No one will take what is mine. I shall defend it until my last breath leaves my body. And so shall you."

"Father," broke in Edward, who had been silent until then. "No one could ever doubt your courage or your service to the King, but there are those who feel that your claims to the land you took from neighbouring lords are weak. There is talk of false ownership and the use of extreme force in taking the lands."

As Edward spoke, his father's face grew red with rage. "You dare to speak against your father?" he interrupted. He raised his arm, his muscles rippling against the pull of his clothing. "Shall I remind you of your place, boy?" he threatened, his fist ready to strike.

But Edward stood strong against his father's anger. "Alas, Father," he continued, "I regret to be the one to tell you of the taunt now used against you by your enemies. They call you Kenrick the Brute."

A roar erupted from Nora's father, quieting the murmurs of the knights. Above in the gallery, Nora held her breath. Everyone waited for his fury to burst forth. But Kenrick bellowed with laughter.

"Let them call me Kenrick the Brute," he gloated. "I think I like it much. It will do to inspire fear in my enemies. As for claims of false ownership of the land for which I justly fought, this matter I will take up with the King's council." Then to Edward he added, "You do well, Son, to inform me in such matters."

"So, my lord," asked another knight as he held up the message, "how shall we meet their challenge?"

"With strength and cunning," answered Kenrick. "Our success will depend on our defences. Battle in open country would show the weakness of our numbers. No, we shall make them come to us. The castle defences are strong, but we must prepare ourselves."

He began to give orders. "You, summon all available men to the castle. Appoint sentries along the wall and send spies into the forest. Report the movement of all enemy troops. You, ensure we have a good supply of water and food, and throw all who cannot fight out of the castle. Ration the food supplies and prepare for a long siege. The rest of you instruct the garrison to prepare the weapons. I will call the priest to bless our battle and pray for our cause."

A slight cough drew attention to the gallery above the great hall.

"Who dares to spy on my council?" Kenrick's voice boomed against the castle walls.

Thoroughly frightened now, Nora first tried to make herself invisible. Then she fled through a nearby doorway, chased by the sound of her father's footsteps on the stairs.

She ran through a small storage room stacked with chests toward another chamber. She pushed aside a drape that covered the entrance to a larger room with painted red and white walls, a fireplace, a stool and a washstand. Nora climbed into a huge four-poster bed with heavy curtains around it and pulled the quilt up over her head.

Moments later, her father thundered into the room. He travelled the distance from the door to her bed in only a few steps.

"Eleanora," he growled, "you dare to spy on my council? Have you no respect for your father?"

Nora lay still on the bed, refusing to answer.

"I give you gifts, food, a husband. And still this is not enough? What say you, Daughter?" he persisted. "Have you no tongue—no defence for your actions?"

Without waiting for a response, he brought the full strength of his fist down upon her. The jewels in his many rings sliced deeply into her cheek. And yet Nora did not cry out.

"Next time, I think, you will know better," he said as he left. "Remember, girl, no one spies on my doings."

Nora wept softly into her pillow. Her red hair had fallen across her face in loose wavy strands. Tears streamed down her face, mingling with the blood on her cheek.

I couldn't help but drop the key then. Nora's pain was my pain—her blood was my blood. His fist against her cheek felt as if it had struck my own. And I let go of the key.

With surprise, I noticed that evening shadows had started to gather in the corners of my bedroom. The photos of my mother on the walls were faint and ghostly, and my stomach grumbled with hunger.

But my thoughts were still with Nora and her father. Why had he hit her? He truly was a brute. Much worse than my own father could ever be.

Then, feeling an ache in my cheek, I wondered if I too had been injured somehow. I pressed my fingers against my cheeks and felt dampness, but my fingers were not wet with blood, only with my own tears of sympathy.

Stumbling over to the mirror, I examined my reflection. I looked grey, like my father, and, for the first time, I could see his features in my own face. But there was something else, something even more disturbing. There, on the same spot where the rings had cut Nora, my own crescent-shaped birthmark throbbed with her pain.

13

STEDMERE

I can't remember Duncan ever being late for school. But that day, Duncan threw himself into his chair just as the school bell buzzed. I only had time to whisper hello before Mr. Fahim, our math teacher, began to speak.

"Open your books to page 50, everyone. We're going to take up problems 1 through 10."

I groaned—I had forgotten all about my homework last night.

While Mr. Fahim talked, I sneaked a quick peek at Duncan. He was flipping through his textbook, looking for the right page. He had done his homework, but he looked awful—as if he hadn't slept all night. His face was pale, and his eyes were dark and heavy, but he was almost vibrating with excitement.

I thought that something was wrong, so I

passed him a note. "What happened to you?" I wrote.

Duncan scribbled a reply. "Stayed up to look for castles! Scored big!"

After that, I couldn't wait for class to end. The hands on the clock seemed to move ever more slowly until they almost stopped.

When Mr. Fahim finally did finish with us, Duncan jumped up right away. Then the words fairly spilled out of him.

"You should've seen the castles I found last night!" he burst out. "There are some great sites out there. I found this one place that lists tons of castles, with maps and photos of each one."

"Great! We're sure to find Nora's castle now. But I have something to tell you, too."

Duncan knew right away what I was talking about. "You held the key again." He sounded annoyed, as if he resented being left out of that part of our adventure.

We walked together down the hall to our next class. English, Room 12. I told him that I had seen Nora listening in on her father and his knights, and that her father was preparing for a battle. I also told him how Nora's father had whacked her hard across the face.

"He hit Nora," I said simply. "It was awful. Her father stormed into the room and he hit her so hard..." I couldn't finish. Such violence between family members was beyond my experience. On TV, maybe, but in real life?

Duncan was horrified. "Was she hurt?" he demanded.

"Of course she was hurt. Afterward, she lay crying on her bed. And her cheek was bleeding all over her pillow." I shuddered at the memory of it.

"What happened next?"

"He warned her not to spy on him and he left." Then I showed him my birthmark. "See this? My birthmark is in the same spot where Nora's father hit her!"

"Yeah?" Duncan peered dubiously at my face.

"And last night it was throbbing with pain." Duncan still looked doubtful, but I kept going. "And I have something else important to tell you."

I was about to tell him that we had a name to help us with our search—Kenrick the Brute—but just then I noticed Ms. Tanglemoth. She was standing in the doorway to one of the classrooms, hiding slightly inside. She was close enough to hear my every word.

"I wish I could see the castle too," Duncan complained. "I want to see what you see."

"Shh. Ms. Tanglemoth is listening," I whispered. She knew that I had the key and she wasn't demanding it back. Instead, she was keeping a close eye on my every move.

"What? You've got to be kidding..." Then Duncan spotted her, too. "What is she doing? What could she expect to learn from us?"

"Good questions." I pulled Duncan down the hall. I wanted to put some distance between Ms. Tanglemoth and us. "And we might get some answers—after we find that castle. You see, I didn't tell you the best part. We now have a name too, a name to hunt for. Nora's father was called Kenrick the Brute. Maybe we can find out something about him."

We barely stopped long enough to gather snacks from Duncan's kitchen before we headed to his room. We both wanted to find that castle, and the sooner the better.

"This is what I wanted to show you," began Duncan when he found the site he had told me about. "There are hundreds of castles listed here. Just look at them all!"

"Wow. It's going to take us a while to look through all of these."

"I searched through as many as I could last night," said Duncan.

"I could tell," I interrupted. "You didn't look exactly bright-eyed this morning."

"Yeah," muttered Duncan. "Like I was saying, I searched through them but I couldn't find one that seemed just right. But then, I've never actually seen your castle. That's where you come in."

"Okay. I'm sure I can recognize it. Let's go. We have no time to waste." I was eager to start.

"Great. But it's not as easy as you might think. A lot of these castles arc falling apart. Sometimes nothing's left but a pile of rocks."

"No problem," I said with confidence. "Let's do it."

Together we scanned picture after picture for a glimpse of something familiar. Duncan had marked a few that he thought were close, but I kept shaking my head. As supper hour grew closer, I became more and more restless.

"We have to hurry. I don't have much time," I said. "My Dad will be all over me if I'm late again."

"Just call him," suggested Duncan. "Tell him you're working on a project at my house and you're staying for supper. My Mom won't mind."

"Great plan," I agreed. "But let's just check out a few more castles first."

"You look. I'll go tell my mother. Be back in a minute." And he was running down the stairs and calling out to his mother. "Mom! Can Moon stay for supper?"

At that very moment, I saw it—the Great Tower. Weather and time had turned the white walls into dull grey slabs. The tower still looked solid, but it was somehow weary—tired of holding itself erect for so many hundreds of years. Moss had gathered in the rocky crevices. And before it stood the remains of the gatehouse. It was unmistakably Nora's castle.

I couldn't speak to call Duncan back. I could only stare at the computer screen. Stedmere Castle. It was called Stedmere Castle. I was so happy just to know its name. Our search was over. Finally we would get some answers.

"My mother says it's cool," began Duncan as he came through the door. He stopped when he saw the expression of amazement and satisfaction on my face. "You found it," he stated simply.

I only nodded as Duncan rushed over to peer at the screen. "Are you sure? Does it look absolutely right?"

"Oh, yes. I'm sure. This is it," I replied quietly. I stood up restlessly and began pacing the room. "Stedmere Castle," I whispered to myself. I still couldn't quite believe it, but saying its name out loud helped make it more real.

"Wow. There are photos, a map and even a virtual tour." Duncan began to read the description. "It says here that it's located in a remote area of northwest England. They think it was built in the thirteenth century."

We both read the text on the screen. "Once a massive structure that proudly ruled the countryside, Stedmere Castle is now only a shadow of what it once was. Jagged chunks of stone litter the inner and outer courtyard. There are several breaches in the walls, and the ramparts and guard towers have collapsed in many places. Only the gatehouse and the largest tower appear more or less intact."

"What are you kids doing up here?" interrupted Duncan's mother. "Didn't you hear me calling you?"

We both jumped at the sound of her voice.

"Oh, sorry, Mom. We were really concentrating."

"I can see that," answered his mother. "Well, it's good to see you so interested in this project you're working on, but it's time for supper. Moon, I assume you've called your father already?"

"Uh, no," I stammered. "I'll do that right now."

"You'd better hurry up. He's probably getting worried by now. I know I would be," said his mother.

Never had I gulped a meal so fast. The food was delicious, but I was too eager to learn more about Stedmere Castle to enjoy it. I wolfed down a tomato salad, noodles heaped with shrimp in a cream sauce and butter tarts for dessert. Somehow it was fitting that such delicious food should come out of Duncan's kitchen. Perfect food for a perfect family—so different from the fast-food dinners I shared with my father.

Duncan's parents asked us about the project. I answered as briefly as I could, without mentioning anything about magic, keys or visions. Duncan interrupted when the questions became too difficult, and for once we were grateful when Kirk started talking baseball.

When dinner was over, Kirk left for a game and, with our stomachs full, Duncan and I raced upstairs. We bumped against each other, laughing to see who could get there first. But we settled down right away, anxious to learn more about Stedmere Castle.

"Let's see what the machine has to offer," said Duncan.

"An excellent site for a castle because of its natural defences," we read, "there is, in fact, evidence that Romans occupied the site long before Stedmere Castle was built. An invading force would have had to attack up the steep hill on which the castle sits, traverse a deep ditch, which has since been filled in, and assault the soaring walls. Invasion from the north was impossible— the hill turns into a sheer cliff that falls sharply to a river, thought to be quite wide and deep during the Middle Ages.

"Legend has it that the castle was the site of a devastating siege. The story is that Kenrick of Stedmere—lord of the castle in the time around 1250—was a cunning, ambitious man. He annexed the lands of neighbouring lords with great force and cruelty, earning him the nickname Kenrick the Brute. In time, his enemies united against him to lay siege to the castle. The siege was bloody, as both sides were enraged with bad blood. The attackers eventually won entry to the castle through treachery from within, killed all they found, fired the outbuildings and looted the castle."

"Kenrick the Brute!" I yelped. "I told you that was his name! Now we have solid proof that the magic of the castle key is for real!"

"Yeah." Duncan stared at the screen, amazed. "I figured you must be telling the truth, but now..." And we both got lost in reading again.

"The gatehouse and Great Tower remained garrisoned by the victors for a time. Then the castle was abandoned. It currently belongs to the Crown, which has done nothing to maintain or restore it. With so many castles in England that are better preserved and less remote, few tourists ever visit Stedmere. Even today, the area around the castle is sparsely populated and tourists will see only rolling hills and a few small cottages. The nearest town is in the richer and more hospitable valley to the south."

Duncan leaned back in his chair and folded his arms across his chest. "This is definitely the castle. There's no mistaking Kenrick the Brute."

"Yeah, we found it," I grinned happily. "The question is, what do we do now?"

"I know just what to do." Duncan's voice rang with confidence. "We touch the key again. Did you bring it?"

"No. Of course not. What if Ms. Tanglemoth had gotten hold of it?"

"Then let's go to your apartment and get it. I wouldn't mind having another try at it."

I could hardly trust my ears. At first Duncan hadn't believed in my visions. Now he was itching to use the magic key himself. He had come a long way.

14

THE SIEGE

The TV in my apartment was blaring so loudly that we could hear it from the hallway. Once inside, we saw that Dad had pulled the beige curtains shut so that the apartment was dark and gloomy. He lay slouched on the living room couch with his feet up on the coffee table.

"Hi, Mr. Arlette." Duncan was too nervous around my father to say much.

"Uh, hi, Duncan." Dad was surprised to see him, but at least he wouldn't complain about my being late with Duncan there.

"We're going to my room," I muttered toward Dad. My father and our apartment felt as shabby as usual, and I wanted to escape to my room.

Dad turned back to the TV, which was blasting a family sitcom. A mother, a father, three kids and a dog. They were all eating supper together at a table, except the dog. And they were laughing.

"How can he stand to watch that happy family stuff now that Mom is gone?" I wondered to myself.

I stood there a moment watching the show. When I couldn't take it any longer, I turned without a word and marched down the hall to my room. I knew Duncan would follow me.

Once there, I carefully removed the key from its hiding spot as Duncan swung his leg over my desk chair and sat backward on it.

"You hide it under the mattress?" Duncan was surprised. "Everybody in the movies always hides things there!"

"So, it's still a good place," was all I said. That happy sitcom was still bothering me.

"Okay. Sorry. Can I still have a chance to touch the key?" Duncan's eyes were hopeful, and I could understand his longing.

"Sure," I answered, trying not to sound angry. And I unwrapped the key.

It lay on the royal blue cloth in my hand, daring me to touch it. I really wanted to touch it, but I had promised Duncan. Without another thought, I passed it to him.

"Here goes." Duncan grabbed the key.

I shut my eyes and wished hard that Duncan would be able to make the magic work. I wanted to give him the best possible chance.

Maybe I didn't wish hard enough. Or maybe Duncan didn't want it to work. Or maybe the magic wasn't meant for him. I don't really know. But I do know that, when I opened my eyes again, nothing had happened. Just like before. No trance, no distant gaze. Duncan couldn't make the key work.

"It's not fair," Duncan almost shouted.

"Shh." I pointed toward the door. "We don't want him in here."

"I've heard all your great stories. I want so much to see Nora and the castle myself."

"I know." But I was thinking about the key. I knew its magic would probably still work for me—that it wasn't broken—but I wanted to make sure.

"Let me check that the key still works," I said.

Duncan still held the key, but with a big sigh he passed it to me. I grabbed it, shutting my eyes tightly with relief as the tingling magic of the key moved through me. I was back in the castle again.

Shafts of morning sunlight slid across the great hall. Kenrick was seated in his massive chair to one side of the unlit fireplace. Nora and her mother sat on the other side, each drawing out, twisting and spinning her own unbroken thread of wool from a long stick onto a spindle. Her mother's face looked drawn and sad. Nora's face was thinner, bored and listless. The air hung like walls between them.

Five knights marched in. They were in full armour, carrying their helmets under their arms. Chain mail with metal plates was fastened overtop. Swords and daggers hung from sturdy belts.

Nora's father stood as they pounded across the floor, his eyes narrowing into slits of suspicion.

"I did not send for you," he grumbled.

"My lord," began one of the knights. He was the largest one—almost as tall as Nora's father. His voice was low and gruff, and he smelled as if he hadn't bathed in a year. "The food stores are low. We have missed both planting and harvest. We have been holed up inside these walls since spring. We cannot last the winter."

Kenrick's body tensed like a cat about to

pounce, sensing the danger around him. Then he spoke carefully, firmly. "You have promised me your service. And you will be faithful until I, or death, release you. Each one of you will defend this castle until his last breath."

Another knight stepped forward, I recognized him as Madoc, the knight who had escorted Nora back to the castle.

"No," Madoc growled. "The pledge that we swore no longer holds us. You cannot feed us. Too many have died already in sorties and now the rest of us are starving. The bond is broken."

Kenrick was strangely silent, although his red face betrayed the anger that was building inside him. But he was alert, watching the others carefully. Judging them. Plotting his next move.

Then he spoke. "You know that the biggest dangers during a long siege are starvation and treachery. There is food enough to keep us alive. I have carefully rationed the food and posted my most trusted men to guard it. You will not starve. But do not cross me or you will suffer a traitor's end."

Nora's mother hunched over, her eyes on the floor. Nora watched her father and the knights with frightened eyes.

"They have sent a messenger," began the large knight, gesturing with one hand. But Kenrick refused to let him speak.

"What are you suggesting?" he roared, throwing a cup across the room. "That I surrender to these devils? They killed my only son! Captured and paraded Edward in front of the castle. Made sure that I saw him before they lopped off his head. Then, as a final injury, they killed the rest of the men that I had sent out with him through the secret tunnel. Edward was to bring us supplies and reinforcements. It was a masterful plan! Instead, he is murdered. Dead. Even my daughter's bridegroom, Gilbert, was murdered. Eleanora widowed before she was even wed! No. These castle walls have withstood their attacks. We will not give in to the threat of hunger."

At the mention of Edward's name, Nora's mother began to sob. Nora's eyes also filled with tears. But she held them back as she carefully watched the knights and her father.

Madoc spoke next. "The message says if we surrender, all lives will be spared. That Nora will be wed to the son of Artus, who waits outside to take control of the castle. You might yet see your daughter ruling here in Stedmere Castle with Artus's son."

Nora gasped.

Her father shot her a look that silenced her. "They have plans for my castle—my castle and my daughter! Will they cart me off to a tower prison? I am to agree to this!"

"My lord, these are good terms."

Nora stomped her foot. She tossed her auburn hair and threw her chestnut-brown cloak over her shoulders, exposing the sapphire-blue brooch at her neck. I could barely make out the faint scar on her cheek, a mirror to my own birthmark.

"You would marry me to an enemy?" she asked forcefully. The brooch seemed to glow brighter with her words.

"Nora," whispered her mother sternly, pulling her back. "This is not for you to decide."

But Nora broke free. "How can you say that?" she reproached her mother. Then she turned to her father and the knights. "You talk about me as if I were stone."

"Enough insolence," yelled Kenrick in a voice that could shake the walls. "I am lord of Stedmere Castle. I will decide what you all will do." He glared at Madoc and the others. "And, you, Eleanora, will marry whomever I choose."

Nora stood frozen for a moment. Then in one wild movement, she broke away from the group and rushed for the exit. She raced down the spiral stone staircase, leaving behind her father's anger, the knights' rebellion and her mother's indifference.

She hurtled down to the lowest floor of the Great Tower. In a storage room piled with chests and weapons, she huddled in a corner, head on her knees, sobbing uncontrollably, until her tears ran dry.

Without warning, the sound of war horses pounding, kicking, stomping in the courtyard penetrated her refuge. The clash and roar of a battle, pierced by screams of the dying, echoed down the stairway. Nora fled up the stairs to the great hall, but it was empty. Only a few ragged servants were desperately searching for places to hide.

"Father! Mother!" she called. But her voice rang hollow off the castle walls. "What is happening?" she moaned.

She ran up the stairs to the gallery above the great hall. No knights stood at the narrow window slits. Peeking from the window, Nora saw that the castle grille was raised high, and horsemen were pouring into the outer courtyard. Only a traitor could have opened that route. Kenrick's men could not stem the assault.

Then the slam of a thick wooden door echoed throughout the castle tower. "The escape door!" Nora gasped.

Nora fled back down the stairs through the storage room to a passageway on the far side. This led to a stout wooden door. She tugged on the metal handle, but it would not budge.

"Open the door!" she screamed, tugging at the handle.

But no one answered.

"Please, let me through!" Nora pounded on the rough wooden planks until her fists were raw with slivers.

Moments later, the invading warrior found her. The sword in his hand was red with blood and his breath was fast and hard. He took off his helmet and stared at her with savage eyes. Then he laughed wickedly, through cracked and broken teeth.

When he spoke, his voice came out in a growl. "You have lived to see twelve winters, Eleanora of Stedmere. But you will live to see no more."

Nora's face was pale with fear. A shiver passed through her as she pressed herself against the door. Then fear left her as she found the strength to stand tall and face her death. The sword pierced her chest. The knight shouted. Nora gasped then slumped to the ground. The intruder pulled his sword free and wiped it on her cloak. Nora lay still, not moving, not breathing, her red hair encircling her head. I knew she was dead.

Duncan's face was close to mine, and he was bouncing questions off me. I could see his lips moving, but no sound penetrated my reeling mind. I pressed my hands against my temples, urging the pounding to stop. "Nora is dead. Nora is dead." My blood pounded to the beat. I sat with my head down for several minutes—until I remembered the key.

"Where's the key?" I struggled to say.

"Relax. It's over there." Duncan pointed to my desk. "Safe and sound."

I sighed and melted into my bed. Duncan just stared at me, waiting for me to tell him what had happened. When I finally recounted this latest great adventure, he blurted out his astonishment.

"She's dead? Dead!" Then he stopped. "What does that mean, Moon? How do we find your mother now? What do we do next?"

"What we need is more information," I said, sure of my words. "Information that I'm betting only Ms. Tanglemoth can give. We need to talk to her."

15

SECRETS

I knew the rumours about Ms. Tanglemoth—I had started a few of them myself. She was the leader of a coven of witches who practised black magic. She could cast a spell over kids to control their every thought. She had been born hundreds of years ago, but because of the evil in her heart she could never die.

After so many days of hiding the key under my mattress, I carried it to school the next day in the left pocket of my jeans. Ms. Tanglemoth didn't seem to want it back. So I was going to take it to her and ask her for help.

Duncan was nervous, not sure of my plan. "I don't like having anything to do with Ms. Tanglemoth," he said, his voice crackling with tension.

But I thought I knew what I was doing.

"We're just going to ask her for help. That's all."

When we ventured into the library after last class, Ms. Tanglemoth waited for us behind her desk. I felt like a fly risking the spider's web.

I stopped in front of her desk and faced her narrow grey-brown eyes. Duncan halted two steps behind me.

When she saw us, Ms. Tanglemoth stood behind her desk—still as a telephone pole in a thunderstorm. Even the glasses that swung on the chain around her neck didn't move. As if someone had pressed her pause button.

"Ms. Tanglemoth, do you know a lot about castles?" I asked. I wanted to see her reaction. If she had seen Nora's castle, that might give me an opening.

Ms. Tanglemoth remained still and calm. She seemed more machine than human.

"If you want to research castles, check row three, third shelf from the top," she answered flatly.

Duncan shifted uneasily behind me.

"Ms. Tanglemoth, did you ever notice anything special about the key—the one I took from you?" I tried to keep my voice down so the kids at the checkout desk couldn't hear me. There was no point in telling everyone that I had taken her key.

Ms. Tanglemoth marched around the desk toward us. She folded her arms tightly across her bony chest, the wrinkle lines around her mouth and eyes suddenly twisting into a deeper scowl. She reached a bony hand out to me and said, "If you need to ask, then you're not up to the job. Give it back to me."

"What? Give you back the key!" My mind was racing. Surely she couldn't mean it—not now!

She held her hand level with my nose. "I thought you were better than that, really. Thought you had some magic in you. But I guess you're no better than the lot of them. No, give it back. Not yours to begin with."

One quick glance behind me at Duncan told me that he was going to be no help. His lips were tightened into a forced smile and his eyes were blinking open and shut like a camera shutter snapping a string of pictures.

"No, I can't give it back. I left it at home," I lied feebly.

"Don't try that on me, Moon Arlette. You know very well that key is in your left pocket right now. So give back what you can't handle."

I stared at Ms. Tanglemoth, hardly believing her words. Her eyes, usually so cold and hard, showed something different. Her chin tilted up proudly. Her lips were almost fighting back a smile.

It was my turn to look bleak, dreary, grim. The little voice inside my gut told me to give up all hope of finding my mother. My eyes were fixed on Ms. Tanglemoth, unable to break free. How could I give her the key? I couldn't imagine giving it up. But she knew I had it. She had read my thoughts. My body was numb, but I felt my hand reach into my pocket to protect the key.

Then without a word, Duncan came out from hiding behind me. He stood beside me, facing Ms. Tanglemoth. We were two magic novices pitted against one powerful witch. But we would not back down.

I decided then that I would not give up the key. I would run. I would go into hiding, if I had to, but I would not give up the key until I understood its connection with my mother.

But my feet were firmly fastened to the worn dull-brown carpet. I was not going to run. Instead, I found the words to plead with Ms. Tanglemoth. One last try at reaching through to her.

"I'm sorry that I took your key without asking. It was wrong. But when I touched that key I saw a castle and a girl with red hair—although Duncan didn't see anything. And that girl looked so much like my mother. You see, my mother's disappeared and I want to find her. Ms. Tanglemoth, can you help us understand the mystery? Did you ever see a castle or a girl with red hair when you held the key? Please?" I held my breath waiting for her answer.

"Your mother left in your thirteenth year?" wondered Ms. Tanglemoth, almost to herself. "Not a surprise. They always leave."

"Who always leaves?"

Ms. Tanglemoth looked at me hard—up and down. Like she was checking out a piece of fruit in a supermarket.

"I had hope for you, Moon. I thought that birthmark on your cheek was a sign of your power. Thought you had a chance. But I don't know if you're strong enough."

"Strong enough for what?" I held my hand to my cheek protectively.

Ms. Tanglemoth sighed then and muttered, "Not in my nature to help. The curse holds me from it."

"The curse?" She wasn't making any sense. But my body was tingling with excitement, almost the same feeling as when I held the key.

Ms. Tanglemoth looked at me hard again. Then she examined Duncan too. She seemed to arrive at a decision.

"Come," she ordered us.

She spun on her heels and headed quickly toward the back of the library, taking the corners around the bookshelves sharply. Duncan and I followed, almost racing to keep up. We were an unlikely parade. Suddenly, she stopped at the orange, metal door to the back room. She pulled her band of keys from her wrist and unlocked the door.

16

CURSED

Duncan edged into Ms. Tanglemoth's back room beside me. I guess his curiosity was stronger than his fear. Ms. Tanglemoth strode to her desk, opened one of the side drawers on the desk and began thumbing rapidly through file folders. I was still a little dizzy with surprise at being invited into Ms. Tanglemoth's back room.

Everything was as I remembered it— empty storage shelves, stacked boxes, a low counter and sink. Ms. Tanglemoth's desk had been cleared of papers, but the photo of the black cat was still there. I nudged Duncan and pointed to it. He nodded. Then I pointed to the shelf beside the desk.

The wooden box that had contained the key was still there, as well as the photos. I wanted a closer look at the photos, but Ms. Tanglemoth spun around, several fat file folders in her hand. Her eyes were brighter than I'd ever seen them, and her face was flushed. But she was still scowling at us.

"Come in. Shut the door." She gestured for us to move closer.

Duncan closed the door, but didn't let it click shut. Then he followed me a step or two toward Ms. Tanglemoth's desk.

She placed the folders on the far side of her desk and sat down on the only chair in the room. It was a creaky old desk chair with wheels. Pulling herself up to the desk, she selected a pad of lined paper and a blue ballpoint pen.

"If I'm going to help you," began Ms. Tanglemoth, "then you'll have to be honest with me. Tell me everything you experienced when you touched the key. And everything about your mother."

I tried to give her an exact account of our doings—magic and otherwise, but Ms. Tanglemoth was impatient and insisted on the strangest little details.

"Really, you are a most imprecise girl, Moon. Did your mother leave before or after your twelfth birthday?" she inquired sternly.

Then she asked me about the time of day my mother had disappeared, about the note she had left and if my father was still around. She wanted me to describe every detail of every castle vision. And she wrote down every word.

It all made me feel a little uncomfortable, especially the part about whether my father had left too.

"Why do you want to know this?" I asked.

But Ms. Tanglemoth just gave me "the look"—an icy, warning stare—and I gave up trying to understand her reasons.

Finally, Ms. Tanglemoth put down her pen. She tore off the pages she had filled and filed them in one of the folders, which she patted with something like contentment.

The squint lines around her eyes deepened as she focussed on Duncan and me. Then she said sharply, "I have something to show you. Listen carefully, and don't interrupt."

Neither of us ventured a peep, but I felt a thrill of anticipation. I pushed up the long sleeves of my sweater to cool down.

"The key could never work for Duncan, no matter what." Ms. Tanglemoth spoke with grave exactness. "It wasn't meant for him."

I glanced at Duncan. At the mention of his name, his forehead had wrinkled anxiously. Or maybe he was disappointed that the magic couldn't work for him?

"It was only meant for members of our family, Moon."

I jumped. Our family? I had never met anyone from my mother's family. Could I be related to witchy old Ms. Tanglemoth?

"Yes, Moon. Your mother—she is my half-sister. Our father had two families—first mine and then your mother's. And with both of us, our father left us in our thirteenth year of life." Ms. Tanglemoth spit out her words in short, clipped bursts.

"Here." She stood up to reach for one of the photos on the shelf.

Ms. Tanglemoth passed me the photo, and I held it so Duncan could see it too. The frame was black metal, and the glass covering the picture sparkled, clean of dust or fingerprints. In the photo was a young girl, about my age with flaming red hair and deep brown eyes. She looked much like my mother, but the nose was a little too pointed and the face too narrow. Standing on either side of her, with their arms resting on the girl's shoulders were a man and a woman.

"This is me, with my mother and father," Ms. Tanglemoth said. "You'll see the family resemblance."

Then she pulled open one of the file folders.

"And this is your mother with my father and his second wife."

I gaped in stunned silence at the second photo. I had seen only a few pictures of my mother as a girl, but this girl looked just like Nora.

"I have researched the whole family genealogy—our descent through history." Ms. Tanglemoth shuffled papers on the desktop. "Of course, there are many holes and inconsistencies, but I have traced the family quite far back. Very far back. And I'm fairly certain that we are related to Eleanora of Stedmere Castle. The girl you know from the castle key. The story is that her parents, Kenrick and Helena, escaped during the attack on the castle. They fled to France, where they began a new life and had other children. We are descendants of this second family, Moon."

I stared at diagrams of family trees. Uncles. Cousins. Aunts. Great-great-grandparents. Heat rushed to my face. Blood pounded through my body. Still, I could not speak. But I could feel Duncan beside me. His hand was on my arm, steadying me in a stormy, rocking sea.

"The key has been passed down through the family. It came to me from my uncle, my father's brother, after his death. He knew me to be an organized person, so he trusted me with his papers—many of which are hundreds of years old. I have letters, notes, wills and so on. Most recount similar events. The same stories over and over. Parents abandon their children in their thirteenth year. Or they become so withdrawn and distant that they may as well have left. Families are divided by betrayals too deep to mend. Some talk of a family curse. Many are sure that the family has had some sort of spell cast on it. Fact or fiction, I don't know. But there are numerous stories like that in my files. And I have collected even more evidence. Like yours."

"Mine?" I asked, my voice high and shrill.

"Don't you see, foolish child?" Ms. Tanglemoth snorted. "This is why your mother had to leave and your father is as good as gone. And this is why I let you take the key from me in the first place. Because you wouldn't have listened if I had just told you about our family history. I had to let you find the key. Lead you to it and let you find your own way to Nora and our troubled past. Don't think I haven't heard your talk that I am a witch. I know." Her mouth tightened into a stubborn line.

I thought then of the many rumours I had spread about Ms. Tanglemoth myself, and I felt a spurt of shame.

"So now I give you one final challenge," she continued. "Keep the key. Take it home. Not that it will help you much. You've seen all you need to know if you've seen Nora's death. There's no more to tell. But you must try to lift the curse. Do something to end the suffering of this family. It is too late for me. And I have refused to have children of my own. So I am passing the burden on to you. And if you fail, you must pass the key on to the next generation."

"Okay," I answered, glad that the key was mine to keep. A gift from an unlikely relative.

"I've made copies of a few things from my files." She passed me one of the file folders. "Family tree. A few letters. Just so you remember the important details. I don't want you to lose interest. You're young for a task like this, but there is no one else."

Ms. Tanglemoth gathered the papers on her desk, tapping them into a neat pile. She slid them back into the drawer.

"Well, that's it," she said suddenly. "I've had my say. Go away now."

"Okay. Uh, thanks, Ms. Tanglemoth." I clutched the folder to my chest.

Duncan and I shuffled toward the door, heavy with our new knowledge.

"By the way, Duncan, the magic may not work for you, but Moon very much needs your help." Ms. Tanglemoth waggled a long finger at him.

Duncan shook his bangs down in front of his eyes. "Yes, Ms. Tanglemoth."

Then Duncan and I made our way out of the library together. Too surprised for words, we moved in silence.

17

THE CHALLENGE

We sat in the shade of a huge oak tree at the front of the school and leafed through Ms. Tanglemoth's papers. The stories were the most interesting I'd ever read. The old black and white photographs showed people sternly posing for the camera, the girls in long dresses and formal clothes. They looked so foreign I could hardly believe they were my relatives. But sometimes the shape of a face or tilt of a chin told me that these people were indeed my family.

And the letters. Round, swirling script that was hard to read. More recently there were typed notes. All hinted at the same problem. Time and again, families were torn apart in the thirteenth year of a child's life. It was eerie. Their stories were so similar to my own.

"Wow. Ms. Tanglemoth did a lot of research," marvelled Duncan. Then he added, "Moon, do you think there really is a curse?"

"I don't know if I would call it a curse." I flipped over a photo to read the names on the back. "But something weird is going on in my family. There's a terrible pattern, repeating over and over again. Maybe it is caused by magic, maybe not. That doesn't really matter."

"How can you say that?" Duncan handed me back a stack of photos.

"What does matter is that we put a stop to it. Maybe we can use magic to do that. But how?"

The wind picked up then and ruffled the top papers, threatening to scatter them across the schoolyard. I shoved them back into the folder and tucked it carefully into my backpack. Then we headed for home—it was close to suppertime. But we both agreed to think about what to do next. We would meet after school the following day.

As I trudged toward my apartment building, I debated showing the photographs and letters to my father and telling him about our experiences. I could even show him the key to see if he could make the magic work. After all, he was family.

But I wasn't sure I wanted to do that. He didn't seem to care about much these days, so how would he understand this?

When I closed the apartment door behind me, I still hadn't decided what to do. But Dad wasn't home yet, so I had a few minutes to myself. I could try the key one more time. Maybe I'd see something new— something that even Ms. Tanglemoth didn't know about.

I sat on the couch in the living room to unwrap the key. I picked it up hopefully, but this time I was in for a disappointment.

The magic still worked. I did have a castle vision, but it was a replay of the first one, Nora and Madoc riding together toward Stedmere Castle. The scene unfolded just as before. I knew what they were going to say and do.

Ms. Tanglemoth was right. I had learned all I could from the key.

Then I heard Dad's footsteps in the hall. He always walked with heavy, even steps. So different from my Mom, whose walk was more like a dance step, but light—as though she were hardly touching the ground.

I ran to my room to stash the key under

my mattress. Only this time I slipped the file folder under there too.

When Dad began banging pots around in the kitchen, I joined him there and sat on one of our two kitchen chairs. I shoved my hands under my legs and watched him heat up some canned spaghetti. My hands stuck to the plastic of the chair.

Dad knew that I was in the kitchen, but he didn't say anything. Not even hello.

"What's new?" I asked him to start the conversation.

Dad frowned into the pot of spaghetti.

"Nothing good," was all he said.

"I had a surprising day." I hoped he would ask me about it. He just reached for plates and cups from the cupboard above the sink.

After he had buttered bread and sliced some cheese, I asked, "Aren't you going to ask me about it?"

"What?"

Dad looked at me with surprise—then his eyes and face went blank again.

"You weren't even listening, were you?" My muscles clenched into knots.

"Not tonight, Moon. I've got problems at work. I don't need to get it from you too."

He scooped the steaming spaghetti onto the plates and carried his into the living room.

I wondered. Was he acting this way because of the curse? He didn't look like someone controlled him from outside. But maybe this wasn't my real Dad. Maybe the curse caused him to be so distant. If that were true, then maybe I could win him back, as well as contact my mother.

I decided then not to tell Dad about anything. I would work it out with Duncan. Dad was too far gone, but maybe I could help him.

The next day at school Ms. Tanglemoth didn't come near us, and we steered clear of her. Not that I was afraid of her any more. There just didn't seem to be anything else to say to her.

After school, Duncan and I wasted no time. With me perched on the back of his bike, we reached his house in record time and rushed upstairs to his room where we could share our ideas in privacy. I told him the castle visions were just reruns, and I wasn't sure what to do next. But Duncan had a plan he wanted to try.

"I've found a spell to break any curse that may be acting against you." He was excited and proud of himself.

"Where did you get it?"

"I was playing around on the Internet last night. Looking for ideas. And I came across this."

He fished a neatly folded sheet of computer paper from under a pile of books and papers on his desk and handed it to me. It was a print-out of a recipe to cancel a spell. I read the whole thing carefully, while Duncan looked eagerly over my shoulder.

"I'm not sure this is the way to go," I said finally. "I think whatever we do should have something to do with Nora. She appears in all the castle visions. And her parents left her when she was about twelve too. I think this whole thing started with Nora."

"It might have. But we don't really know for sure." Duncan was disappointed. "I think it's worth a try."

"We don't even know if there is a curse..." I began. Then I stopped.

I hadn't seen Duncan so excited about doing magic before. There was a change in him. He was determined, focussed.

"Okay. We'll do the spell," I agreed.

"We have to do just what it says." Duncan began reading the paper. "Put a tall white candle inside a bowl. The white candle stands for new beginnings."

Duncan had gathered together all of the objects we needed. Sitting across from him on the floor, I followed his instructions.

"Stick the candle to the bottom of the bowl with some wax. Fill a separate container with spring water."

"Where are we going to get spring water?" I asked.

"Use this bottled water." Duncan jumped to his feet and reached for a bottle on his dresser. "The label says it's spring water."

"Good enough." I stuck the candle in the bowl and opened the bottle of water.

Duncan watched me, then he continued reading. "Light the candle. Imagine the spell against you is flowing into the white candle. Feel the purity of the candle clearing any ill will from you. Say, 'Let all spells against me now cease to be.' Then pour the spring water over the candle's flame. When the flame sputters out, the spell will be broken."

"Okay. Let's try it."

We had tried spells like this before, but until the wishing spell, nothing had worked. I did my best to focus on the candle flame and to do as Duncan had instructed.

When the flame finally fizzled out, Duncan asked, "So what do you think? Do you feel different? Did anything happen?"

"No," I answered. The whole thing hadn't felt right to me. But I didn't want to admit that to Duncan.

"Maybe it will take a few days," he suggested.

"Maybe."

"There is one more thing though. We have to throw away the candle and pour out the water. This will scatter any remaining negative power."

"You go ahead. I'll wait here," I said.

"Oh, come on, Moon. You've got to try harder." Duncan got to his feet and waited for me to follow.

But I knew it was useless to finish the spell.

"Just saying a spell won't make it work." I tried to say it so Duncan wouldn't get upset. "You have to feel it. It has to be from the heart."

"How do you know I didn't feel it?" he said with an edge in his voice.

"Neither of us did. It just wasn't right at all. I can't explain it."

"I can. You just weren't trying," Duncan said.

"That's not it at all." Duncan didn't understand me, or magic, very well. He didn't know how to listen to the voice inside—that soft voice that tells you what feels right. "We have to stop trying so hard. Then it will happen. Magic happens when you relax into a deep place inside yourself. And the spell doesn't come from the Internet. It's just something that comes from inside. We're going about this all wrong."

"Wrong?"

"Yes, wrong." Then I had an idea. "That's it. Duncan, do you have a blue candle? I have an idea. And we'll need a piece of paper too. And we'll use your computer to go to the Stedmere Castle site online. To the virtual tour. That will help us to imagine that we're really there."

"Where?"

"Inside Nora's castle."

18

THE GHOST

Some things I do make no sense to anyone, especially Duncan. Even I don't understand why I do them. But I just know that I have to. It's hard to explain. It's like I'm walking down my street—the same one I walk down every day—when all of a sudden I see a path that I hadn't noticed before. And I just know that I have to walk down that path. Even though it may change me forever.

Duncan left his room to pour the water down the drain and bury the candle in his parents' garden. He wanted to finish the spell. When he came back, he brought a small blue birthday candle.

"This is all I could find," he shrugged. "But we had good luck with a birthday candle before."

"It will work great," I assured him. My

ideas were coming to me fast, and I was filled with their energy. "I took some paper from your desk. Can you take us to the Stedmere Castle site?"

Duncan pushed a button on his computer. With a quiet hum, it powered up. He cleared the desktop and dragged a second chair over for me.

"So what are we doing?" he asked as he sat down and his fingers clutched the mouse.

I pulled the key, still wrapped in its cloth, out of my pocket. Unfolding the cloth, I set the key flat on the desk in front of the computer screen. Duncan had already found the Stedmere Castle site.

"First I'm going to write Nora's name on a piece of paper. Then I'll set everything up." I wrote her name and folded the paper under the saucer with the candle.

"Why did you want a blue candle?" asked Duncan.

"I'm not sure really. It just felt right." Then I thought about why. "Blue is for healing. And it is the colour of a sapphire. Nora has a blue sapphire brooch just the colour of the ring my mother gave me—the one I lost on the day that she left. And there were the flashes of blue light that I saw during the wishing magic. There are a lot of reasons."

"Are we going to touch the key?" Duncan asked.

"Yes. The key is our connection to Nora. But I want to do more than just see another castle vision. We have to connect to her somehow. Because I think she is the source of all this trouble in my family. I think we need to heal her."

"How can we heal her? She's dead, Moon." Duncan shook his head.

"We're not trying to bring her back to life. We're going to heal her spirit," I explained. "Her parents betrayed her—left her in the castle to die. Maybe that was the beginning of the pattern."

"So what are we going to do?"

"I want us both to think about Nora. Try to picture her the best you can from what I have described to you. Dark red hair. Large blue eyes. She looks like the photos of my mother as a girl. Remember?"

"Okay," Duncan said. "Then what?"

"Then we'll imagine how we can heal her." I finished arranging the key, the candle and the paper on Duncan's desk. "Everything's set. You can light the candle now."

Duncan lit the candle and started the virtual tour of the castle.

Images of a decaying Stedmere Castle flashed across the computer screen. Like Duncan, I let the sights wash over me for a moment. The key glowed dimly in the soft candlelight and the computer light.

"Okay," I began. "Imagine Nora in the Great Tower moments before her death. Her parents have just left through the escape door, locking it behind them. And Nora is trapped in the castle. She can hear the enemy knights fighting in the courtyard. She feels betrayed, abandoned. Try to see everything in as much detail as you can."

Duncan listened to me, staring at the computer screen in front of him. He was focussed. His eyes like big saucers were seeing only inside himself.

"Can you see it?" I asked.

Duncan nodded but didn't break his concentration.

"Now we're going to send her all our positive energy. Give her some strength to fight back."

I felt I had to say something else then, so I searched my thoughts for some special words that I could say for Nora. I finally came up with a kind of spell.

As I spoke it, I could feel Duncan break out of himself and look at me. But I just stared ahead, pushing aside my doubts and centring on the ruins of the castle, the blue candle's flame and the dull metal key.

> *"As we send this energy,*
> *Your pain will disappear,*
> *Shrivel with your sadness*
> *And shrink away in fear.*
> *Your emptiness will be replaced*
> *With something fresh and new,*
> *A circle of protection*
> *Will forever surround you."*

I don't know how long we both sat there, sensing the pure magic we had worked together. After a while I felt I was spinning, and it didn't feel good. I tried to steady myself, but everything was twirling around me. The flame, the key, the grey and broken rocks of the castle.

I let the spinning carry me for a moment, then I whispered hoarsely to Duncan.

"Okay, Duncan," I said. "We need to touch the key. Let's do it together. Ready? One, two, three...now."

As our fingers wrapped together around

the key, a magic tingling passed between us. It was different from other times when I had touched the key alone. Duncan's power was working with mine—we were growing stronger together. I was pulling him into the magic, using his energy to help us both grow stronger. I knew Duncan felt it too, because his face showed a spark of surprise then glazed over with shock.

Then Duncan was suddenly gone from me. I was moving through a spinning tunnel lined with pictures—like memories of dreams. But these weren't my own memories. They were flashes of thoughts, feelings, images from other people. My mother. My father. Ms. Tanglemoth. And others too. Distant relatives that I had only seen in photos. It was a roller-coaster ride into the past.

I was whirled through these spinning pictures, like riding in the front car of the roller coaster. I couldn't reach out to hold on to anything. It was a dizzying feeling.

My only hope was to aim for the end of the tunnel. I focussed on the place I was being pulled to rather than the spinning images around me. Then I felt more in control—as if I were steering the ride.

I felt Duncan then, although I couldn't see him. But I knew he was there too, seeing what I saw, feeling what I felt. And I knew that he had finally done it. He had found the magic inside himself.

The ride seemed long, although I had no choice but to continue. Finally, the end of the tunnel was in sight. And I came into a space, a stillness.

I saw the white undamaged stone wall of the Great Tower of long ago. The wind was wailing around the outer wall that lined the top edge of the tower, which was outlined against the purple evening sky. I could sense a glow about the castle. Something was different.

Then I saw a spark of life, a focus of energy on the uppermost battlements of the tower. It was Nora. At least, I thought it was Nora, but she was not the girl I had seen in my visions. She glowed a silvery-white—as if she were formed from light. I could see right through her to the stone wall beyond. And I knew I was not seeing Nora, but some part of her that had lived on after her death.

Was this the ghost of Nora? The illusion felt so real that I tried to talk to her. "Nora? Can you hear me?" I called.

But Nora was too distant, too removed. My words were fleeting—they disappeared like wisps of smoke before they could reach her ears. Our worlds had crossed briefly, but we could not communicate.

Nora's ghost was huddled against the rock of the tower wall. A wave of long hair fell loosely across her face. Her face shone feverishly.

"Father!" Nora called out to the clouded night sky. "You did this! You condemned me to die in this castle tower! You may not have held the sword that killed me, but you guided it toward my heart!"

A misty rain began to fall, but Nora didn't notice.

"I curse you, father." The ghostly light pulsed more strongly. "You and all that follow after you. May your heart be pierced with deadly venom, as was mine."

"The curse!" My thoughts were bubbling furiously. "Ms. Tanglemoth was right. There is a curse. And Nora's spirit cast it over seven hundred years ago."

Then Nora's ghostly form fell against the

tower wall. She remained slumped over for what seemed like an eternity, until the clouds parted for the moon, full and round.

Faintly, a plaintive voice came to me through the darkness. "Oh, Edward. Who will help me now?"

19

RELEASED

As Nora's shade flickered against the highest wall of the Great Tower, a new idea took form in my mind. A pinprick of thought at first, it quickly grew into a course of action.

"The key," I thought. "Her parents took it with them. If it could show me Nora and her world, could I return it to her to unlock the escape door? The door that Nora's parents had closed behind them, locking her into her death?"

I couldn't ask Duncan to advise me. Our minds were wandering separately through this magical ride. But these visits had changed, strengthened me. I was surer of myself and of what I could do, and I sensed that Duncan and I, though unable to speak, were still connected in some strange way. So I sent him my idea in thought.

"Duncan, send the key to Nora."

Then I focussed all my energies on achieving my goal.

"Send Nora the key to unlock the door,
Free us all from this curse forever more."

I formed a mental image of the ghostly Nora at the top of the Great Tower, with the key shining in her hand. Not the dull, worn key, but a new one. I concentrated with all my might until the glowing key appeared in her hand. I knew without a doubt that she had received my gift.

Nora's face began to shimmer with an inner light. Her eyes glowed warmly and her pale cheeks seemed to blush a soft rose colour.

She opened her hand and stared at the key in her palm.

"The key," she whispered with wonder in her voice. "Could it be?"

"Yes," I thought to her. "Open the door."

"A key for a locked door. A key to undo the past." Her wonderment echoed in my mind.

Suddenly her glowing form began to move, all the way down two flights of stairs to the passage beyond the storage room.

She stopped abruptly in front of the arched wooden door—the escape door.

Nora carefully slid the shaft of the key into the keyhole. It fit easily, but turning was harder. For a moment, I was afraid that it wouldn't turn. But with a loud click, the bolt unlocked, and Nora pushed the door wide open.

Instantly, a blazing light sliced a trail through the darkness. It was not a warm light, but a cool blue light that looked as if it would freeze rather than burn. It shone with such brilliance that I could see nothing else through the open doorway.

"A heavenly light," Nora breathed.

Just as Nora moved to merge with the light pouring through the doorway, another form appeared out of the mysterious radiance. It was Edward.

"Nora." He smiled and wrapped his arms around her. A ring of light surrounded them both.

Then, without another word, Nora passed with Edward through the doorway and dissolved into the light.

With a painful jolt, I found myself back in Duncan's room. A heavy rain lashed at the window, and I remembered the day so long ago when magic had first worked for me. The computer screen was glowing a murky green—the tour of Stedmere Castle was long over. My head whirled with images. The candle had burned out. My hand was empty—I had let go of the key.

Slowly, I pieced together what had happened. Nora's ghost. The curse. The key. The escape door.

I turned to Duncan. "You did it," I started to say. "This time you felt the magic too."

But Duncan nodded silently. His body rested limply against the back of his chair, but his face wore a wide smile, and his eyes, usually so muddy, were clear golden brown and lit with joy.

"And we sent the key to her," I continued.

Duncan only nodded again. We were both struck into an amazed silence.

Without thinking, I picked up the key with my bare hand but flinched immediately. I didn't want another castle vision or a repeat of an earlier one. I was just too tired. But I didn't feel anything special. There was no magic tingle through my body. No bewildering dizziness that placed me in another world.

"Duncan!" I cried out. "Touch it! The magic is gone from the key."

He placed his palm over mine. "I guess our magic adventure is over. I wonder if we did lift the curse."

Finally, I came back to reality enough to check my watch. Late for dinner again, and it was still raining heavily outside.

"Duncan, lend me a jacket, will you?" I said anxiously. "Rain or not, I've got to get home fast or I'll be in real trouble."

Wordlessly he reached into his closet for a jacket. He pulled out the same jacket that he'd loaned me on that long ago birthday outing. As I stuffed the key and cloth into the pocket, my fingers touched something hard.

"Do you always keep stones in your pocket?" I joked as I brought it out to show him.

But it wasn't a stone. Instead, lying in my hand was a sapphire ring just like the one I had lost the day my mother left.

I gasped. "Duncan, my ring!"

I held it closer. Silver, with a large blue sapphire. My birthstone—my lucky stone. Then I checked the inscription.

"Choose belief over doubt," it read.

"But I'm sure I felt in those pockets a hundred times!" insisted Duncan.

I was too happy to care. I held the ring close and felt the tears in my eyes. I remembered my mother's words on the day she gave it to me.

"Wear it every day for protection," she had said. "It will ward off evil and bring you good fortune."

I slid the ring onto my finger.

"Now that I have it back, what will happen?" I thought. "Will my bad luck vanish and my mother return? And what about my father? What will he think when he sees the ring?"

Then, strangely, Duncan began to laugh. Little bubbles of laughter at first. Then his whole body began to shake as wild hoots escaped from his belly.

I stared, confused, but his laughter infected me until I was grinning too.

"Maybe Ms. Tanglemoth dropped the ring in that jacket," Duncan said between snorts. "Maybe she's a magician."

"We're the magicians now," I added more seriously.

Duncan nodded as he got his breath back. "Why couldn't Ms. Tanglemoth do what we did? Why couldn't she lift the curse? Can you explain that?"

"Not yet," I said, my body aching from the effort of the last couple of hours.

Suddenly I knew what the tiny words on my ring meant. "Choose belief over doubt." If I believed in something, I could make it happen, with a little work. Duncan and I had believed, and we had made it happen. We had freed Nora from her castle walls and I had my ring back. I could do anything.

I splashed happily through the puddles all the way home.

20

CHANGES

As I swung open the door of my apartment, I sensed right away that something was different. To begin with, the TV was off. The place seemed brighter, and I smelled paint.

I wanted to run down the hall to the living room to see what was going on. Instead, I forced myself to hang my backpack up on a hook. I wanted to do this right. Talk to my Dad. Show him the ring. Tell him what I hoped—that Mom would be coming home soon. Maybe even tonight.

When I had peeled off Duncan's wet jacket, I couldn't wait any longer. I marched down the hall to the living room to see what was going on.

Dad was halfway up a metal stepladder with a paint roller in one hand, painting over the hateful beige walls. The ceiling glistened with a fresh coat of white paint and already one wall was a creamy yellow.

The furniture was stacked near the window, covered with sheets to protect it from spills. And the curtains were off the window, exposing our humble apartment to the grey eyes of the evening.

"Oh, Moon!" Dad sounded surprised to see me. He glanced around him with a silly look. "Just thought I'd paint the place. Brighten it up."

"Why?" was all I could say. Not that I didn't understand that the apartment needed painting. I'd wanted it painted ever since we moved in. But why now? What had come over my Dad to make him start painting that night?

"I bought the paint a while ago. I wanted it to be a surprise for you, but I never got around to it. Tonight just seemed right." He shrugged. "Do you like the colour?"

"I love the colour. Thanks, Dad." Then I grabbed a paintbrush lying on a nearby paint can. "Maybe I can help." I hadn't forgotten about showing Dad the ring. But just now I wanted to paint.

Dad smiled. It filled his face, wide and warm. His grey eyes sparkled brightly. "You can paint the edges," he said. "I'll do the middle."

We worked together for several hours, until we had changed the whole room from a TV room into a home. We didn't stop for a meal, just snacked on crackers with cheese and a banana. We painted over the fights, the anger, the disappointment. And we even laughed together when Dad accidentally painted my elbow.

By the time we were done, I had paint on my T-shirt and jeans, and Dad had some in his hair. I was glad that there was no school the next day. Exhausted but still smiling, we cleaned the brushes and roller in the kitchen sink. Finally, I mentioned the ring.

"Dad, I have something to show you." I held out my hand. "I found it." Showed him the ring on my finger. Not a drop of paint had spilled on it.

He stared, blinked a few times, confused. Turned his head sideways to check the ring out closely.

"Moon? Is it really the same?"

"Yes."

"Where did you find it? After all this time?"

I had been waiting for this question and was still uncertain how to answer it. Should I tell him the simple version of how I found the ring in Duncan's jacket or about the magic adventures with the key? I didn't think I knew what to say. But I did. "You wouldn't believe me if I told you."

Dad seemed to accept that, at least for now.

I took the ring off and showed him the inscription. He wiped the paint off his hands before picking it up carefully.

"Do you think this means she's coming back?" I asked, my voice full of hope.

Dad handed the ring back quickly. "I don't think she's coming back just because you found the ring, Moon."

He continued washing the tools. He didn't believe. He was changed, but only to a point.

Not me, though. I knew things were different. I was different. Mom would come or call soon. It would happen.

All weekend, I waited for my mother to walk through the apartment door. Every time the phone rang, I ran to answer it. But the one call I waited for didn't come.

Sunday evening, the phone rang again. I sprinted from my room to the kitchen and grabbed the receiver after only one ring.

"Hello?" I said tentatively, hoping to hear the voice of my mother.

It was Duncan. He was so excited that his words came out all in a rush.

"Moon? That you?" But he didn't wait for an answer. "You won't believe what has happened. Or maybe you will. Remember the wishing magic? When I wished for a new computer? I got one. Really! Well, not a new one. My mother bought a new one for her work and gave me her old one. But it's new to me. And you should see how fast it can load!"

"Great!" I answered. And I meant it.

In the past, I might have felt bad because Duncan got his wish and I didn't. But I didn't feel that way then. I was still sure that my Mom would be back in my life soon, and Duncan's news just made me feel even surer. If his wish could come true, so could mine.

Duncan continued then. "I can't explain what happened the other night. Maybe you left some of your magic behind, because things seem different now. I see things in a new way. I don't know how to explain it." Then he changed the topic abruptly. "Did she come home yet?"

"No." I was glad that he asked.

"She will," he said. And I knew for sure then that he had changed. He truly believed in magic and could find magic inside himself.

By Monday, my mother still hadn't shown up, but I didn't become discouraged. I knew I just had to wait. After school, Duncan and I decided to go and talk to Ms. Tanglemoth. To tell her the rest of the story.

As Duncan and I stood together outside the library door, neither of us felt nervous—not like the last time.

"She might have changed," I said. "Everyone else seems to have."

"Yeah, but for better or for worse?" Duncan joked. And I knew he was still not quite comfortable with Ms. Tanglemoth. That's why we were hesitating outside in the hall until Duncan was ready to go in.

"Come on. Let's go." I led the way and he followed.

We both saw the change in Ms. Tanglemoth at once. No one could help but notice. Her grey hair had been released from the tight bun at the back of her head. It fell softly down to her shoulders and curled up slightly at the ends. And her eyes, usually so cold, were inviting—so much like Nora's that I was shocked even though I expected some changes.

"I knew you would come." Ms. Tanglemoth

flashed us a friendly smile.

This was the new Ms. Tanglemoth. She had the same skinny arms and legs sticking out from under her loose cotton dress. The same regal nose, strong chin and high cheekbones. And the familiar reading glasses swung from a chain around her neck. But this was definitely a new Ms. Tanglemoth.

"I suppose I have you two to thank for this?" Ms. Tanglemoth smoothed her dress as she sat down on the chair behind her desk. "How did you do it?"

And we found ourselves telling Ms. Tanglemoth the whole story, the story I couldn't tell my father—a story he wouldn't understand. I was so pleased to be able to share it with someone other than Duncan. Someone who would believe that we could break an ancient curse flung by a ghost—a family member—over seven hundred years ago.

Then I asked, "How come you couldn't do it? Break the curse, I mean? You are magic, aren't you? You always knew what we were thinking."

"I don't have as much magic as you may think," she laughed. "Yes, I can hear people's thoughts, if they don't block me out. But I'm not a witch, if that's what you're asking. As for the curse, I think I couldn't break it because it had too strong a hold over me. It had eroded who I was, worn me down over the years. By the time my uncle gave me the castle key, I was too weak to stop it."

"That's why you let Moon take the key?" Duncan asked. "Because she hadn't fallen under the power of the curse yet?"

"Yes. And I knew you could help her, Duncan. I didn't have a friend like you to help me." Ms. Tanglemoth beamed at him. He looked surprised.

Then Ms. Tanglemoth turned to me. "Have you heard from your mother yet?"

I shook my head doubtfully. When would she come?

An announcement over the loudspeaker interrupted us. "Moon Arlette. Would you come to the office, please? Moon Arlette."

Duncan, Ms. Tanglemoth and I exchanged looks. Ms. Tanglemoth smiled warmly again.

"Better go, Moon. Someone's waiting for you."

But first I had to do something. I shoved the key into Ms. Tanglemoth's hand. "This is yours," I said quickly. "Sorry I called you a witch. Sorry for everything."

"But, Moon! Why, I'm speechless!"

I raced from the library and down the hall before she could object, Duncan's sneakers squeaking on the polished floor behind me. Turned right, past the cafeteria. Left to the office. Swung open the brown wooden door. And saw my father, waiting for me. My mother was nowhere in sight.

I tried not to look disappointed.

"What is it?" I asked Dad. "What's happened?" Dad had never picked me up from school before.

Dad looked at Duncan as if to say he should go away. Private family business. But I said, "You can say it in front of Duncan. Just tell me."

"Your mother called me at work today, Moon. She's coming back." Dad's dress shirt was glaring white, starched so clean it hurt my eyes. Tears filled me up as I studied his face to make sure it was true. His eyes were clear, though brimming with tears. I heard Duncan gasp and felt him pat me softly on the back.

"Oh, Dad." I whispered, taking a really deep breath for the first time in months. Since the day my mother left.

Dad put a firm hand on my shoulder. "I know what you're thinking, Moon. Don't get your hopes too high yet." His voice was full of caution. "You'd better put a brake on them for now. She may be coming back to town, but that doesn't mean it'll be like before. She's going to stay in her own place at first. Not with us."

But it didn't matter. Mom might not be living with us right away, but I would see her again. I had known she would return, and it had come true.

"Don't worry about me, Dad. It will all work out. I just know it will."

I wrapped one arm around Dad's waist. Now I could hardly wait to tell Dad the whole story. I wanted him to hear about the key, about my step-aunt Ms. Tanglemoth, the castle and Nora. Everything. And Mom, too, when I saw her. Maybe now they would really believe me.

KAREN KROSSING was born in Richmond Hill, Ontario and grew up in the same area. She first became passionate about writing in high school. After studying English in university, she spent the next ten years working as an educational book editor.

Karen loves books about magic and secretly believes that magic is real. She likes wilderness camping, exploring new worlds on the internet and travelling. She currently lives with her husband and two daughters in Toronto. *The Castle Key* is her first novel for children.

If you enjoyed this book, you'll also like...

THE GREAT LAUNDRY ADVENTURE

by Margie Rutledge
illustrations by Maxine Cowan

Faced with a laundry crisis, the Lawrence family buys several new baskets that become gateways to their family's own history for Abigail, Jacob and Ernest and lead to adventures that may threaten their family's present-day existence!

$8.95 in Canada, $7.95 U.S.   ISBN 0-929141-67-9

A CIRCLE IN TIME

by Peggy Dymond Leavey

Twelve-year-old Wren finds a mirror that shows her reflections from the past of the silent movie era in her Ontario hometown. In the past, she makes an unlikely new friend and witnesses the making of a legendary film with such oddly familiar actors...

$6.95 in Canada, $5.95 U.S.   ISBN 0-929141-55-5

9790043